THE
GUARDIANS

HEATHER JONES

Published 2021 by Heather Jones

Compiled and Distributed by DoctorZed Publishing.
10 Vista Ave
Skye, South Australia 5072
www.doctorzed.com

ISBN: 978-0-6450012-2-8 (sc)
ISBN: 978-0-6451840-9-9 (ebk)

A Cataloguing-in-Publication entry can be found at the National Library of Australia.

Cover design © Open Book Howden | openbookhowden.com.au

Printed in Australia, UK & USA

rev. date: 14/04/2021

THE
GUARDIANS

HEATHER JONES

For Bert

CHAPTER 1
The Night
June, 1970

Zipping through the night like a shadow, the little black sports car was one with the dark, shiny, rain wet streets and the vibrant colours of reflected neon. Brian Moore was on his way home and in a pensive mood.

The victory dinner with his colleagues had been lively and amusing. In his first year with Syms Simcock, Barristers and Solicitors, Brian's input into the Carson case had been minimal, so to be included as one of the successful team felt good. Capping off the evening was the surprise arrival of his housemate Mike with his new girlfriend, Amanda. Dropping into the restaurant for a late supper,

Mike was equally surprised to see Brian.

Lawyers, especially young ones, when celebrating, are a convivial lot and as Mike's girlfriend was simply spectacular, it was no surprise they were invited to join the party. A good party man, and quite at home with those that remained of the victorious diners, Mike was happy to join in. Amanda flirted with everyone at the table, delighting them all and proving again, men are universally silly in the company of a pretty young woman.

Brian was glad to see them both. As the first evening of its type, in his experience, he was determined to see it through to its end, although it was beginning to pall. Mike and Amanda gave the occasion a refreshing spark. Brian knew being seen in such company, cast him in a new light.

His colleagues only knew him as a steady worker who rented a house with a friend from university. Now, he could sense his work mates speculating as to what went on in that house, and wondering if Brian had a collection of spectacular girlfriends too. Brian smiled to himself. If only it were true. Girls swarmed around Mike like bees to honey, around Brian they buzzed off. Not that Brian minded, he wasn't attracted to, nor did he want a collection of spectacular young women. He was yet to discover his ideal, when he did just one would do. If he was envious of anything, it was Mike's ability to fall in and out of love so often, without causing hurt or rancour.

'He is probably making love to Amanda at this very moment,' he thought slowing down as he approached the intersection of George Terrace and Palmer Street.

Stopping at the lights he noticed the absence of traffic; it was as if the city was deserted. There were only two girls on the other side of the intersection, they were turning into Palmer Street, although, he thought he saw a movement in the shadows some fifty or sixty metres behind them.

One of the girls wore a long dark coat, the other a furry jacket, micro mini-skirt and knee-high boots. Sensing danger, Brian put his car into gear. Almost simultaneously, the figure of a man emerged from the shadows, rapidly moving up on the girls. The one in the dark coat swung around abruptly to face the stalker, the other kept on walking.

Not waiting for the lights, Brian slammed his foot down on the accelerator. Engine roaring, horn blaring, he charged across the intersection, pulling up with a loud screech of brakes.

'Are you alright?' he shouted, scrambling out of his car, eyes on the presumed attacker who was sprinting off. The girl too was intently watching the retreating figure of the man and said nothing.

'Are you alright?' Brian called out again and the girl seemed startled at being addressed. She turned toward him, taking a few steps into the brighter light to see him more clearly. She was equally illuminated, and Brian found himself looking into the most beautiful face he had ever imagined. Whatever words he had been going to say died on his lips. She showed no sign of fear or alarm, only surprise at his presence. He stood mesmerised for several moments while she scrutinised him closely.

'Yes, thank you,' she replied at last, her voice as pleasing as her appearance.

'Your friend left you to it!' said Brian, still unable to take his eyes away from her.

'She's going to her car,' the girl answered. An engine starting up sounded in confirmation, then the unmistakable sound of a car driving off, caused Brian to turn his head.

'She's leaving!' he exclaimed in astonishment, turning back to the girl. She was gone.

Amazed, he turned around in full circle, looked up and down the street, walked around his car. Hurrying to the corner of George Terrace and Palmer Street he found no sign of the girl, no people at all. Once again, he noticed the city was deserted. He ran back down the other side of Palmer Street, checking in the same manner, stopping when he was opposite his own car.

An old dark building with a 'For Sale' sign on it, sandwiched between two tall office blocks, stood there, directly opposite his own parked car.

'I should have looked here first,' he muttered, moving into its deep shadows without hesitation. Searching thoroughly, calling out, and trying the lock on the gate of the service lane at the side of the building, all with no result. She was nowhere to be found.

Back in his car he caught the merest wisp of a lovely fragrance, but that too was gone before he could inhale any of it deeply. It upset him, almost as much as losing the girl.

Very reluctantly back at home, quite some time later, after having driven up and down Palmer Street many times, he still couldn't settle. Taking a shower and going to bed made no difference. Restlessly he got up, walked around the house checking rooms, including Mike's.

There was a feeling of not being alone! Checking the rooms again, looking out of windows, peering into every dark corner of the garden, the feeling persisted. Sitting in the one good lounge chair, he leaned back his head, closed his eyes and tried to visualise her face. Nothing happened, until he caught another breath of that fragrance. He sat bolt upright;

eyes wide open. The room was empty. Totally void; and he in the middle of it knowing now, that he was absolutely alone. Tiredness came suddenly and an overpowering desire to sleep.

Mike found him next morning still seated in the chair, mentally confused.

'Hey!' said Mike with his usual good humour, 'what happened to you?'

'I don't know,' Brian replied vaguely, 'I must have had too much to drink.' Letting himself down in front of colleagues was disappointing, it sounded in his voice.

'Don't worry!' said Mike cheerfully, 'you were OK when I left, so you can't have been too bad. Now they will know you're only human!'

Brian smiled grimly. There was a greater concern, an inner conviction of something precious lost! It was to do with an old house in Palmer Street, but he didn't want to speak about it because it hurt. It really hurt. Taking a cold shower, he decided, would help him think better. He resolved to go back.

In daylight the area looked much different. There were no office blocks and the only likely old building didn't look dark or shadowy. No 'For Sale' signs appeared anywhere in the street. Convinced it had all been a dream he determinedly put it out of his mind.

Only the sense of loss lingered.

CHAPTER 2
The New Girl
June, 1980, ten years later

Helen Gilbertson, closely followed by Charles Briers, Managing Partner of Syms Simcock, a very reputable law firm in Adelaide, returned to her office in a state of shock.

'Did you see what I saw?' Charles asked of Helen, his Office Manager, who was stressed for many reasons and couldn't answer.

'He's due in court in about ten minutes and there he is fussing around a total stranger, as if nothing had happened!' Charles sat down in the visitor's chair. He wanted to be briefed.

About an hour ago all hell had broken loose between Brian Moore, a partner of the firm, and his secretary. She was the third new girl appointed for Brian in as many months and Charles was fed up. This morning's ruckus had resounded from one end of chambers to the other. It was loud enough to draw Charles from his rooms.

When Helen appeared on the scene with a complete stranger in tow, he was in time to witness Brian's temper dissolve.

'Well!' said Charles, waiting for a reply. 'What's going on? You were in the thick of it!' Generally pleased with Helen's staff management, Charles' only reservation was that she was inclined to like people with strong personalities. Today's incident was a good case in point. Anyone could have seen this latest girl was unsuitable for Brian. To be fair, Helen could have been beggared for choice, never-the-less, disappointment darkened his features. Helen was making a mess of matching up Brian with a secretary.

'You were right, of course,' Helen began, noticing his mood and attempting to mollify him, 'I wish I had listened to you. The girl took every criticism personally and has been concentrating on the wrong things, leaving urgent matters undone. A complete breakdown of communication! Brian discovered what was happening, blew his top, she quit. Now he's in a fine mess.'

'So, who is the girl with Brian now?' demanded Charles.

'She's from the Agency,' Helen lied. She didn't know from where the girl came, but couldn't tell Charles that, she was already feeling sick at the thought of what she had done. It was too late to pull back.

'How did she get here so quickly,' Charles was puzzled. He needed more information. It was not easy to replace staff, certainly not in a matter of minutes.

'Simple good luck,' Helen replied. I phoned the Agency as soon as the row blew up. They had this marvellous, newly registered secretary on their premises, so they sent her around straight away. It's not far as you know. I went downstairs to meet her and you know the rest.' Helen listened to the lies falling off her lips and felt ashamed. Charles had been kind to her. She was from outside the profession and trying to establish a new career. He had given her a chance and was generally supportive.

'It took us all by surprise when you walked in with Ashley..., I didn't catch her surname.' Charles was starting to feel a little easier, the Agency were reliable.

'Preston,' Helen replied gruffly, at least that was the truth as she knew it.

'I thought Brian recognised her,' Charles mused. 'Did you?' he queried.

'Perhaps he did,' Helen partially agreed, 'there was something. It could have been recognition,' she was relieved to get the conversation back on safer ground. 'He didn't know her name though, perhaps he's seen her somewhere.'

Helen was feeling anxious, she really must get the situation with Ashley straightened out. She stood up, hoping Charles would take the hint. He did, rising immediately.

'Let me know how things work out,' said Charles as he left the room, 'I'll get my girl to help.' Charles never volunteered the services of his secretary. Helen was almost too amazed to thank him.

Hurrying back down the passageway to Brian's rooms she judged that by this time, he would have left the building, and she could speak to the girl alone. There were two other people in what was now Ashley's office. They were from Administration, sorting out the first things to be done. Ashley appeared to be comfortable, asking and answering questions from both girls in a clear soft voice, looking up and smiling as Helen entered. Then Suzy, Charles' secretary came in, and there was no opportunity for a private chat. Muttering something about coming back later, Helen left, deception weighing heavily on her shoulders.

She had not contacted the Agency for a secretary. There simply had been not enough time. While trying to catch up with the departing girl she had come face to face with Ashley. Helen couldn't remember their conversation. Like someone mesmerised, Helen ushered Ashley upstairs past curious staff straight into Brian's office, without so much as asking one question. Brian was angrily stacking files into various heaps when he saw Helen at the door.

'This is entirely your fault!' he accused, the words dying on his lips as Ashley stepped forward. Surprise suspended the look of anger on his face. There was a flash of recognition, of memory struggling to emerge.

'Ashley Preston,' she had said holding out her hand. 'Helen has brought me in to help you.' He took a few moments to reply.

'Brian Moore,' he replied shaking her hand, letting it go reluctantly. There was silence for another few moments.

Helen escaped, murmuring something about letting them get acquainted. In her hurry she had nearly bowled over Charles, who at that time had been hanging around the door.

'How did Ashley know my name,' she worried to herself. 'How did she know about the job? Why did I do what I did?' She felt ill with anxiety.

'Helen!' a cool soft voice called out; Ashley had followed her into the passage.

'Everything will be all right,' she said quietly, 'trust me,' then turned back into her office.

Maybe because she wanted to, Helen did.

CHAPTER 3
The Apartment

E arly morning, several weeks later in the offices of Syms Simcock, Brian Moore stood staring out of his window, his thoughts occupied by Ashley.

Several other practitioners were busy in their offices. The aroma of freshly brewed coffee wafted up the passage from the staff kitchen. A phenomenal increase in business over recent weeks, affecting every section of the practice, seemed to have started from the time Ashley joined the firm. Thankfully she was working for him. Good support staff was essential and he found her quick, reliable and calming. Not once in these past weeks had he lost his temper; a fact not gone un-noticed by the office in general.

In recent months he had been troubled by an inner tension. It was almost as if he had been waiting for something to happen. He acknowledged he was sometimes short tempered and moody. In an effort to shake off that feeling, he had taken on extra physical activity, enlisting the help of his recently retired father to re-design his garden. Usually Brian could talk to his father when they were working together, but this time found he could not.

Ashley's arrival put an end to all that turmoil. She was so pleasant to work with, so nice to look at, so exquisitely fragrant. Curious about her, he kept his curiosity in check. Something stopped him from being familiar. She was friendly in a cool way, but never elaborated on her background, except for what he as an employer was entitled to know. She told him her only previous employer was Forbes Williams QC, in Sydney. She had gone to work for him straight from St. Anne's College.

Helen had been around at the time and pounced on the information, surprising Brian who thought she would have known these facts.

Helen's attitude puzzled him. She was always hovering around, seemingly as fascinated with Ashley as he was, and just as reluctant to ask questions. Memory continued to bother him. Something was there but would not emerge.

Sounds from outside his room told him of Ashley's arrival. He knew her footsteps. When she came in, he was back behind his desk fiddling with papers. Greeting him as she usually did, she took her seat and began flicking through her notebook. She looked lovely in a well-tailored suit and crisp white blouse. Expensive looking clothes, he thought and always in the same conservative style. She always wore her hair the same way too, twisted up into a neat knot. His gaze dwelt on her hair, the most colourful thing about her. A pretty red-gold of the curly type that looked like it didn't want to be restrained. Perhaps that was the conundrum, she was reserved, but her hair suggested otherwise.

Several times he had asked her to join him, the other partners and their guests for 'drinks,' a casual affair held in the board room at the end of each week. It would give her an opportunity to get to know the other staff better, he explained, but she always refused. Never-the-less she was a ray of sunshine from that first day. Everyone had pitched in and helped of course, but she was wonderful, staying on until late that first night to finish a draft.

Sometimes, she looked at him expectantly, and he was at a loss to know why.

He liked their working routine, fifteen minutes each morning sorting through the day's priorities gave him an opportunity to observe her while he tried to unearth that elusive memory. He mentioned it once, but her response was so negative he didn't broach the subject again.

Today he was quick to notice a difference in her manner, she seemed warmer.

'Did you enjoy your day off?' she asked, looking up suddenly and catching his scrutiny. Her eyes were blue and candid. Usually they were blue-grey and distant. It was unusual for her to ask a personal question, and he was embarrassed to be caught staring.

'Yes, thanks,' he quickly countered, which wasn't strictly true. His first full day off in weeks and he couldn't settle to anything.

'Did you know you have blue paint in your hair?' he said, neatly turning the conversation back on Ashley.

She gave a rueful smile as she felt the spot he indicated. It was the first time he too had made a personal observation. She laughed a little, he smiled in response.

'I shifted into my new apartment on the week-end,' she explained, 'it wasn't quite ready, the living-room walls need painting. I volunteered to do them myself and got into a mess. Painting is not as easy as it looks.'

It was an opportunity not to be missed. He discovered she had found the apartment on the morning of the day she started working for him, but couldn't move in because of a building upgrade. He was surprised to learn the building was in Palmer Street in the city, not a known residential area, but close to these chambers. He offered to paint her walls as a special thank you, for all the extra effort she had put in at the office. After some hesitation she accepted. He would have to work late all week to have Saturday free, but could not have been happier.

The proposed working bee brought a new ease to their relationship. They chatted a little each morning, mainly about the new apartment, which she described as one very large room with awkward features, tiny kitchen, tiny bathroom and a lobby. The place had been unoccupied for decades she told him, so she spent her evenings washing things.

When he drove up on Saturday morning, he found the building to be a solid, old red brick construction set between two new contemporary style office blocks. It was the type of place you could pass by and never notice. He drove down a side access lane and parked at the rear of the building in a service area for tenants. There was no sign of life except for the sound of traffic. He found the back door securely locked, so strode quickly around to the front.

At street level two shops flanked the

entrance, one Braithewaite's Antiques, the other Maria's Lunch Box. It was too early for them to be open for business. Set back a few feet from the shops and guarded by columns, the entry housed a heavy wooden door freshly painted black. The fanlight over the door somewhat ironically proclaimed the place to be 'Light House'. An electronic entry panel displayed five apartments. He knew Ashley's to be number one, the others were unoccupied. A lonely place for a beautiful young woman to live he thought uneasily, as he pressed the buzzer and announced himself. He heard the 'click' as the door unlocked, he pushed it open, entered and closed it carefully, finding himself in a rather handsome foyer.

The whole place smelled of paint and there was white dust of building work in progress everywhere. A well-proportioned staircase, its newel posts and balustrade covered with dust sheets, swept up to the floor above. Cardboard was taped onto the steps for protection. Wooden wall panelling, in good condition, lined the body of the foyer.

Ashley appeared at the top of the stairs.

'Brian! Up here!' she called out. She was dressed in old jeans and sweater as he was and looked small against the background of dark timber and building chaos. She looked happy to see him. His spirits lifted in response and he took the stairs two at a time.

'I really appreciate you helping me out like this,' she said sincerely, 'I know how busy you are.'

'Pleased to help,' he replied, 'besides, a bit of real work will make a nice change.' They both laughed easily together.

'Would you like to see around first?' she asked.

'Yes, I would,' he replied readily, for once not having to mask his curiosity.

She showed him the four new apartments. Once inside he saw they were modern and utilitarian, in total contrast to the old-world appearance of the foyer and landing.

'Where is yours?' he asked perplexed.

'Over here,' she said leading him to what he thought was a decorative niche in the centre of the wall space. The recess was about six feet wide and panelled like the rest of the interior. Closer inspection revealed it to be a doorway.

'A secret door,' Brian exclaimed in surprise!

'Hardly a secret,' she laughed, 'the knob and keyhole give it away.'

Opening the door revealed more stairs leading up to another landing. In the corner stood a neatly made single bed. Crowded into the space was a chest of drawers, a moveable clothes rack carrying about a dozen of Ashley's suits, a small table and chair.

'This is the lobby and my temporary quarters,' she explained with a broad sweep of her hand. Brian was amazed. Always so beautifully groomed yet she lived on a landing.

'And this,' she said moving over to and opening another solid wooden door, 'is the apartment.'

He didn't immediately notice the dust sheets and newspapers spread all over the floor to protect the polished surface, or the painting equipment set out in readiness for the job ahead. His attention was completely taken by two plaster angels, standing over six feet tall in the middle of the room.

'These are the awkward features I mentioned,' said Ashley with monumental understatement, 'they are what I have been washing all week. I had to take it slowly so as not to spoil the paint work.'

He didn't try to hide his surprise or admiration. They were beautiful pieces of work.

'Are they yours?' he enquired, still examining them.

'They came with the property,' she explained. She could see by the look on his face he was having difficulty coming to terms with two large angels standing in the middle of her living space. She started to giggle.

'Is it a joke?' he asked quickly.

'No! No not at all!' she replied, trying to look serious and making matters worse.

'What's so funny then?' He was perplexed.

'You looked so dumbfounded, I couldn't help it,' she explained, dissolving into gentle laughter. He regarded her steadily. She had a habit of bowling him over. First when she walked into his office, then when she became friendlier, and now her happy acceptance of living with a pair of large statues. He started to busy himself with the painting gear.

'We better get started or we won't finish today,' he said trying to sound businesslike, but her laughter was catching. It was impossible not to respond, his face creased into a grin.

'You can tell me about those things,' he said indicating the statues, 'as we work.'

They did more talking than painting for the first couple of hours, both of them completely unaware of the passage of time. Ashley it appeared, came across the old building when she first arrived in town and was looking for a place to live. It had a 'For Sale' sign on it which suggested potential residential tenancies.

Something clicked in Brian's brain when the sign was mentioned, but he dismissed the thought as irrelevant. Ashley telephoned the agent and that was how she found her apartment. The agent also told her that in years gone by her apartment and lobby were one room, the inner sanctum of a religious sect, the Angels part of the decor. When the apartment was first partitioned, they were placed in the lobby, overpowering that small space. At Ashley's request, they were moved back into the larger room, after the floor was done. They will be pushed back against the wall once it is painted.

'As soon as I saw the statues, I knew this was where I was going to live, they feel like friends and I am no longer completely alone,' Ashley stated simply.

Brian was at a loss for words again. Could it be she was just cruelly lonely, and that was what endowed her with an air of remoteness and mystery? She is blossoming now he thought, like a bud unfolding and lovely to watch. How sad to think two statues were all she had to call on for friendship and comfort. He wondered why she hadn't befriended some of the girls at work, but then realised there would have been little opportunity; we have all been too busy. He felt guilty for having demanded so much of her time and resumed painting with added vigour.

The day disappeared into evening, broken only by coffee breaks and lunch at Maria's Lunch Box. Alfred and Ernest Braithewaite called in just before the brothers went home for the day. Ashley had purchased the furniture in her lobby from them and they wanted to tell her about a wardrobe they had found.

Brian thought the real reason for their visit was to check him out. They were delightful middle-aged gentlemen, old school, well-mannered and protective of Ashley. Tom and Maria from the Lunch Box were protective of her too, in their own down-to-earth way. It was Maria who arrived unannounced with coffee twice during the day and Tom who came up later to collect the tray. Perhaps the Angels were taking Ashley under their collective wing.

At last the room was finished. They washed up and walked to Ziggy's, a small restaurant not far away, recommended by the Braithewaites and where Ashley had reserved a table. It was late, but not too late for a good dinner, one of Ziggy's special Hungarian hot pots, and a relaxing glass of wine. Too replete at the end of the meal to want any more to eat or drink, too comfortable to want to move, Brian toyed with some wine left in the bottom of his glass. They were both quiet and content with their own thoughts.

'I think we have come a long way today,' he said for no particular reason, other than the words just popped into his head.

'I was thinking the same thing,' she replied, but her voice was distant as if her thoughts were far away.

It was time to go, he decided. He collected their jackets and ushered her out into the cold evening air. She rejected his offer of a taxi home, preferring to walk. They strolled along companionably, laughing a bit about being the scruffiest patrons in the restaurant. He insisted on seeing her to her apartment door.

'You have been so good to me today,' she said unselfconsciously, reaching up and kissing him warmly. 'I can't thank you enough,' kissing again, his surprised but very responsive mouth.

It was the sweetest salute and it hit his

system like a narcotic. He wanted another, wanted very much to return her kiss. It was the hardest thing to deny. Every instinct told him it could easily escalate into the most exciting sexual encounter of his life. Fighting to remind himself that he was her employer, and she alone and vulnerable, he decided it best to take things slowly.

'I've had a really good day,' he whispered huskily, resolutely putting her away from him. 'I'll see you Monday,' and left quickly, before he changed his mind.

CHAPTER 4
The Day

Ashley rose early next morning, dressed quickly and set about returning the painting equipment to a cache of tins and brushes further along the upstairs landing.

'Brian's efforts turned out well,' she thought, a frown coming to her forehead. Painters were contracted for the job, but it suited her purpose to allow him to help. His suggestion presented an opportunity for them to spend some time alone together, and Ashley was getting impatient.

They shared an important bond. It was the reason she came to Adelaide. She wanted to explore that bond, but until her move into Light House, felt in no emotional condition to do so. Despite the makeshift nature of her settlement into Light House, she was already refreshed enough to reach out to him. Now she regretted her action.

Pushing thoughts of Brian away, Ashley wandered back into her apartment. It was upsetting to think of him, so she tidied her bed and collected her breakfast. While her living arrangements were awkward, Ashley made optimum use of Maria's Lunch Box. Six days a week they delivered Ashley's requirements for breakfast, lunch and something to heat up for dinner. Ashley had bought a handsome carved box to house these deliveries, a hall table to set it upon and placed the items outside the door to her apartment. It was like having a personal catering service.

Returning to her make-shift bed-sitter, sipping hot coffee from a mug and nibbling one of yesterday's muffins, she made herself comfortable, letting her thoughts range over the time spent in Light House. Much had been accomplished.

Tomorrow Braithewaite's men would put the Angels into position. White plantation shutters would be installed, and then she would be ready to take delivery of her possessions. Ashley felt a twinge of excitement at the thought of unpacking the goods, half of which she had never seen.

Two containers made up the consignment. One had been in storage twenty-five years. The other contained items inherited from Aunt Ellen and Uncle Max. Both containers would come from Glenbourne, about one hundred and fifty kilometres south of Sydney. Ashley wanted the consignments kept separate, so two rooms downstairs were reserved for storage. Again, Braithewaite's men would assist by stacking, stowing and moving things. The daily inhabitants of Light House treated her like family, and she was grateful. So far all was working out well, Brian was the only problem.

He was exactly as she remembered him. He remembered her too, asking if they had met before, but Ashley needed him to be specific. She could feel his interest and wondered if it was as exciting as her own. All day yesterday he was forthcoming about himself, his parents recently retired, his younger married sister, Susan, his brother-in-law, Gary and their twin little boys. His conversation ranged over a variety of topics, but never once touched on the subject of their bond. Perhaps because of Ashley's previous reticence, he made no effort to prompt her for more information than she was ready to give. Because it was so important, Ashley kept the conversation centred on her arrival from Sydney, her discovery of Light House and anything relevant to that time in her life.

The shrill ring of the telephone cut into her thoughts. She listened to it without moving, waiting for the answer machine to engage.

'Hi, it's me, Brian,' said Brian's voice, 'I was wondering how our job turned out.' He paused a second, 'I have a bit of spare time today, if you need a hand for any reason, I would be pleased to help. Ring me.'

Ashley had no intention of doing that, she had made one mistake and wasn't about to make another. Kissing Brian had been an impulsive thing. It was something she had imagined for a long time. It wasn't meant to be so full, but there are times, regardless of circumstance, nature takes what it wants. His response pleased her enormously. Ashley knew he struggled to restrain himself, and gave him no help. She could feel his body relaxing into the embrace at the same time as his hands were on her waist gently trying to push her away. If ever there was an opportunity to say something it was then, but no word was spoken. For whatever reason, Brian was not ready to acknowledge their bond. Ashley felt seriously mistaken in trying to force things along. Not altogether naive, she realised a love affair between them was ready to ignite. If it did it would hopelessly cloud the issue. First things must come first. Therefore, she would continue working for Brian giving him all the time he needed. No more ill-considered advances would be made, and any attempt on his part to do the same would be squashed. Ashley was committed to staying in Light House. For the time being she would concentrate solely on making it her home.

Several messages were on her answer machine by the time she had showered, changed and left the building. Taking an old-fashioned tram car to a local beach she sat on a bench on the jetty for a long time. It was something she did as often as possible, in fair weather or foul. Water soothed her soul. Later, wandering along the seashore she covered a considerable distance before weariness forced to her sit on the sand to rest.

Adelaide's beaches stretch for miles. Along the beach front are houses, cafes, shops, hotels, bus stops and so on. Some areas quietly suburban, others are touristy. Ashley loved them all. It would have been nice to take an apartment by the seaside, but as soon as Ashley saw the Angels, she knew that was where she was meant to live.

Taking leave of Forbes Williams and his wife Anna had been incredibly hard. They were concerned she would be completely alone, and they queried her decision to move. Brian's existence was never mentioned, it couldn't be, at that time she didn't know his name.

Ashley thought back over her arrival at her Adelaide hotel that first evening, and how she immediately made her way to the hotel swimming pool. Water was her relaxant. It felt good, powering up and down the pool with long, neat, clean, rhythmical strokes. For more than an hour she mentally switched off, barely noticing other guests come and go. Back in her room, she took a long hot lavender scented bath. Water was her comfort. She had worked off her nervous energy in the pool, now she was preparing herself for rest.

Hair dried, dressed in white silk pyjamas, she made a cup of herbal tea and when it cooled added a few drops of Valerian essence. Sipping her tea by the window her gaze had ranged over the city square and beyond. To her right were situated the Law Courts. Dotted around the square were dozens of law offices, promising territory for Ashley who had intended seeking work among them. From her vantage point she could see George Terrace, and knew one block away Palmer Street ran off it to the east. That was where her quest would begin.

Composing herself for sleep, she lay flat on her back, hands clasped just below her breast. Within ten minutes her heart rate slowed and her breathing was barely perceptible. Her first night in the President Hotel had been sublimely restful.

Next morning, dressed in a beautifully tailored grey suit, hair severely restrained in a French knot, she strolled from the hotel and headed toward George Terrace. It had been a glorious morning and it seemed to reflect on the people around. Reception staff, porters and a couple of strangers in the street, all smiled at her.

A short distance along Palmer Street she had seen Light House, just as she remembered it from that night so long ago, including the 'For Sale' sign. To be confronted with the solid reality of the building together with the 'For Sale' sign came as a shock, despite always having believed in its existence. Quick tears welled up in her eyes and it took several minutes to compose herself sufficiently to enter Maria's Lunch Box.

It was a typical lunch-time cafe for servicing office workers in the area, she ordered coffee. As there were no other customers, Ashley enquired about the residential development referred to on the sign. Maria, a bright busy little woman, looked at Ashley, liked what she saw and summoned Tom 'to explain about Light House.'

According to Tom the building had been sold about two years ago. Office suites were originally planned, but the idea was scrapped, because of a glut of office space in the city. In Tom's personal opinion the old building was too expensive to adapt to modern technology. Four modern apartments and the refurbishment of the attic were commenced and partly completed, when work was called to a halt.

'Probably financial trouble,' said Tom, 'and now the place is up for sale again.'

Ashley phoned Richard Martin, the Real Estate Agent handling the sale of Light House, from the cafe. He asked her principal interest in the property.

'Primarily a place to live,' she replied.

Not wanting to waste his time, he informed her rental arrangements could not be considered until a contract on the building was in place.

'Then show me the building,' she said with authority. He made no more objections, and was prompt and businesslike when he arrived at the cafe to give her a comprehensive tour.

It seemed to Ashley the building was asleep. Handsome features, dulled by lack of use, needed to be polished up and given purpose. Downstairs were several single empty rooms, upstairs four half-finished apartments, all waiting. Lastly, following Richard Martin up a few more stairs to the attic, he leading the way because he needed to find the light switch, Ashley felt a pang of anticipation.

Light from a naked light bulb flooded the small lobby, and Ashley gasped as she came face to face with two beautiful plaster angels. Standing about six inches taller than Ashley, they were exquisitely painted, although darkly shadowed with dust and grime. Overcome by a confusion of emotion, Ashley's eyes had filled with tears again.

'I forgot they were here,' said Richard Martin. 'I think they were part of the decor at the head of the stairs and were stored here when work started on the apartments. He was busy sorting through a bunch of keys, clearly not interested in the statues.

'This is the attic,' he said opening the door, 'as you can see, someone previously made this space into living quarters. Work hasn't started here yet.'

Choked with emotion, Ashley could not reply. Silently she wandered around taking in her surroundings. She loved the place! Just as it stood! Its impact was as strong as that of the Angels. Still in original condition, it didn't need major renovation, just freshening paint and new appliances. She wondered who had lived there, and began visualising furniture placements. Richard Martin had coughed discreetly, looking at his watch.

'I'm sorry,' Ashley apologised, 'I was day dreaming. Drawing a business card from her handbag, she wrote her name and phone number on the back and handed it to Richard Martin.

'Send full details of this project, on my recommendation, to Forbes Williams, this is his card. He is an investor, and I think the property will be of interest to him. I will tell him to expect to hear from you. Please keep me informed of developments.'

Ashley then returned to the cafe, ordered some lunch and phoned Forbes.

Interested in the morning's developments, Maria wanted to know if Ashley was going to take an apartment.

'I hope so,' Ashley had smilingly replied, 'it's in the hands of the Gods.'

Part of her quest had been accomplished with surprising ease. The place she was looking for existed and unexpectedly, would provide her with a home. Not knowing what to do next and already feeling in its grip, she wondered if she should just abandon herself to fate. She decided to return to the hotel for a swim. That would clear her mind.

Less than a block away from The President, Ashley noticed a barrister in wig and gown hurry into an office building. It wasn't an unusual sight in this part of the city. Intuitively she followed, finding herself in a foyer of a large building.

Polished granite pillars, polished granite floor, a wall of elevators, a stairwell and a prominently displayed, impressive brass framed 'Directory of Tenants', exuded conservative substance. Ashley stood for a few moments absorbing the atmosphere. Harsh voices coming from the direction of the stairwell startled her. An angry looking, attractive young woman clattered down the stairs and rushed past. Moments later a slightly more senior woman hurried down the stairs. She appeared to be non-nonplussed at finding the foyer empty. Without conscious intention, Ashley stepped forward and heard her own voice say,

'I have come for the position!'

Appearing to be in shock, Helen Gilbertson stared at her for a few moments, but offered no resistance. Leading Ashley into a lift, then through a reception area of a suite of offices, along a passage to a personal suite of rooms, she stood aside allowing Ashley to enter.

His name was Brian Moore, and on him Ashley knew hinged her hopes for the future. He was in a rage, and Ashley smiled at the recollection of his stormy grey eyes sparking with temper, the flush of anger high on his cheeks.

'A man of passion,' she remembered thinking, 'but not often unleashed, judging by the reaction of those around him.' Ashley felt no trepidation as she held out her hand to introduce herself. She too, was numb with amazement at the series of events that had led her here.

Working with Brian was a surreal experience. To all outward appearances it was an ordinary business relationship, but Ashley sensed his attraction to her and wondered if he was aware of her own. She often caught his probing glance, but no reference was ever made to their 'bond.' To have come so far only to be stalled for an unknown reason was nerve wracking, but she steeled herself to maintain a cool exterior.

Adding to her woes, Syms, Simcock was experiencing an unprecedented rush of work, stretching staff to the limit. A spate of noisy, irritating guests at the hotel made a good night's sleep impossible. She considered moving to another hotel, but lacked the energy. The vendor of Light House would not allow anyone on the premises until the sale contract was finalised. That took five frustrating weeks, not an unreasonable time, but to Ashley it seemed forever.

Stirring from her reverie she looked around finding she wasn't far from another jetty and a cluster of shops. Choosing a smart little café, she ordered grilled seafood, salad and a pot of tea. Lonely after the warmth of last night's dinner shared with Brian, she wished he was here and wondered what he was doing.

In the city, Brian was in the office kitchen looking for something to eat. Giving up hope of hearing from Ashley, he had spent the day from early afternoon working in the office. It had taken an enormous effort of will to remain at his desk.

All thought of taking things slowly with Ashley had vanished with the light of day. Wanting to do no more than run with this intoxicating sense of elation, he envisaged taking her on a drive along the coast with the hood of the car down, wind in their faces. Perhaps lunch somewhere, or dinner, or both. Instead, he had been immersed in leases and contracts for the best part of what could have been a glorious day.

Finding a tin of salmon and a few cracker biscuits, he emptied the fish onto a plate, eating it while standing, waiting, for the electric jug to boil. An inveterate coffee drinker, today it didn't appeal. For some reason he wanted tea.

It was always going to be difficult facing Brian Monday morning. As expected, he was waiting when she arrived, the light of pleasure shining on his face until he saw she was her old, cold, guarded self.

Forestalling any comment from Brian, Ashley thanked him again for his help, apologised without explanation for not returning his calls, and for her behaviour in taking leave of him on Saturday night.

'I thought nothing of it,' he lied, in a confusion of disappointment. The truth was he had thought of nothing else.

'Where did you go yesterday?' he asked. The question no more than a cover for his hurt!

'The beach,' she icily replied. He looked at her in surprise but said nothing. Awkwardly they set about their work.

Helen Gilbertson picked up on the brittle atmosphere immediately. Unable to account for her reason for hiring Ashley, she kept a close watch on the pair. Something had happened. There was no doubt Brian was pleased with his new secretary, for that she was relieved. It meant her position was safe. But Brian wasn't safe and that was a worry.

Helen liked Brian, she found him forthright and plain spoken. She knew where she stood with him. Unlike some of the other partners who, if angry with her, would take a more circuitous route to vent their displeasure.

She vowed anew to monitor the situation very closely.

Smooth progress at Light House lightened for Ashley an otherwise tense and difficult time. Her goods from Glenbourne arrived safely and were stowed away. She chose not to examine the old consignment, preferring to leave it until she was more emotionally stable. Max and Ellen's things were familiar and comforting. Selecting what she could use, she contracted Braithewaites to organise their refurbishment. With her apartment rapidly taking shape and no improvement in the situation with Brian, Ashley turned her attention elsewhere.

Shortly after her arrival some weeks ago, she consulted with Christine Forrest, a doctor at a nearby Medical Clinic. The two young women shared an instant rapport. Chatting easily, Ashley discovered Christine could be interested in taking an apartment in Light House. Now that the apartments were almost ready, Ashley invited her around for a private viewing. Conveniently located to her rooms and major hospitals, any one of them would suit Christine's requirements. There was also the added bonus of downstairs rooms being available, giving shape to an idea Christine was considering, that of taking on some private patients.

Another acquaintance rapidly becoming a friend was Maria's cousin Stella Gollo, who rented the Lunch Box's kitchen in the evenings. Stella made popular take-away meals for the Lunch Box.

Almost every evening after work Ashley called in on Stella in the kitchen where, perched on a stool at the big work table, she enjoyed chatting over a cup of tea. Behaviour completely opposite the formal manner she assumed at Syms Simcock. Chris began dropping in too, all three enjoying each other's company. Stella's meals were convenient for both girls, neither of whom were interested in cooking. Conversation was of the moment, work, daily dramas and accommodation.

When Stella complained of the time spent travelling back and forth to Light House each night, it was quickly suggested she move into one of the apartments. Rough calculations on a piece of kitchen paper showed a small financial advantage. The more compelling benefits were time saving, safety issues, taxation benefits and access to city businesses. From working nights on take-away food for the Lunch Box, Stella's business could expand into corporate catering.

Light House was beginning to have a marked effect on Ashley. Unconsciously her blossoming friendships were releasing a long time repressed, natural warmth of nature. It began to undermine her rigid formality at the office. Helping Stella formulate a business plan gave her so much pleasure she thought nothing of asking Brian to recommend a suitable legal advisor for Stella, thereby breaking her rule of allowing him no insight into her life. Startled by the request, he generously offered his own services.

'You are too expensive for Stella,' she honestly replied, 'besides, it's a simple job best done by someone unconnected with me.' It was the first friendly conversation they had shared for more than two weeks; Brian didn't care if she did speak only when she wanted something, it was breaking the ice.

With Stella signed up for an apartment, the three women decided to celebrate by going out together for dinner. A new dress to mark the beginning of a new life seemed appropriate and Ashley began browsing around dress shops in her lunch hour.

Stepping into Medici's, an exclusive after five wear boutique she saw it immediately. Elegant, white gossamer-fine silk, low cut, fluid skirt, designed to tempt a lover. Completely unsuitable for a dinner with girlfriends, knowing she had no immediate use for it, depressingly aware it would very likely never be worn, Ashley purchased it without hesitation.

Back at the office Helen Gilbertson noticed the distinctive shopping bag.

'Medici's,' she exclaimed, raising her eyebrows, 'may I see?' Unable to resist showing someone, Ashley was holding the dress in front of herself when Brian walked into her office.

'What do you think of Ashley's new gown?' Helen asked of Brian. His eyes travelled over it slowly, taking in its glamour and allure, then up to Ashley's face, holding her gaze for a moment.

'Very nice,' he answered briefly, before continuing into his room. 'Where was she going in a dress like that,' he fretted to himself. 'With whom?' Came the sickening question! 'A woman wouldn't buy such a garment without good reason.' His worst fear was being realised. There must be a man in her life! The thought of it made him feel physically ill.

'Brian! Am I right in guessing you are bringing Ashley to Charles' dinner Saturday night?' Helen's voice blundered in on his worries, trampling his sensitivities.

'No!' he snapped. 'What dinner?'

'The one for Henderson's people!' Helen was just as terse, letting her annoyance show. Charles was hosting the evening but Brian was Henderson's lawyer, therefore well aware of the importance of the occasion.

'I'm sorry, I've forgotten all about it,' he muttered in a conciliatory manner.

'Perhaps you could ask Ashley to accompany you,' Helen suggested sarcastically, immediately regretting her spite. After all she was responsible for putting the two of them together and now, she was taunting him.

Brian's eyes flashed with temper. It was bad enough forgetting the damned dinner without it loudly being pointed out he was without a partner.

'I'm not asking Ashley, or anyone else for that matter, I'll be going alone!' His tone of voice should have withered Helen.

'Then perhaps you could accompany me,' she replied, trying to smooth over the little spat, 'I'm going alone too.'

'Whatever!' he grimly replied and turned back to his work.

Five o'clock came around with Brian still feeling aggressively unsettled. Packing up for the day, Ashley sensed his presence standing in the doorway between their offices.

'I suppose you heard your name being bandied about when Helen was here,' he began abruptly.

'Yes,' Ashley replied.

'Would you have come with me, had I

asked?' some devil inside him couldn't let the matter rest.

'No. I have another dinner engagement,' she answered quietly.

'Right!' he said eyes dark as onyx. It was anything but 'right'.

'Would you come for a drink with me now?' he asked that abruptly too. It was a repeat of previous invitations, this time interrupted by the shrill ring of the telephone.

'Brian Moore's office,' Ashley answered. 'Oh! Hello Chris! Yes, I'll be there in about ten minutes. Bye.'

'I'm sorry,' Ashley looked regretful, 'I'm meeting someone in a few minutes.'

'Chris?' Brian asked darkly.

'Yes, Chris.'

Quickly picking up her things, including the shopping bag, she wished him a good week-end and hurriedly left.

CHAPTER 5
The Meeting

Street trees, heavy with bud but refusing to unfurl their promise of spring, looked down on the man hurrying along. On his way back to chambers from court, Brian was taking the long route that took him past Light House. Something drew him to the place and it wasn't the vague hope of seeing Ashley, he knew her to be at her desk in his rooms. Since Charles' dinner, last week-end, Brian had spent as little time as possible in his own office.

Jack Henderson had made the suggestion at Charles' dinner, that Brian work with him from Henderson's premises for a short time. It would give Brian better insight into the contractual difficulties he was experiencing, and help iron out problems associated with his company's restructure. Henderson was a large manufacturer of component parts, his firm like the tentacles of an octopus, reaching into any chink in the economy it could find. Brian agreed for two reasons, it made sense and would distance him from Ashley.

On their way to the dinner, Helen had guiltily confessed the circumstances of Ashley's appointment. She warned that Ashley could be unusually compelling. Still aggravated by the events of the previous day, her comments irritated him further. Turning on her savagely he told her he wanted no further discussion on the matter. They arrived at the dinner in silence, avoiding each other for most of the night. Later on, he told her he would be working out of the office for a few days and would use her to relay his instructions to Ashley. Helen was aware there was tension between them and was happy to comply with any request that would ease the situation.

'What is it that draws me here?' he wondered as he paused in front of Light House.

Its dark facade giving no clue.

Moving on, he thought of the past few months and how they had rushed by full to the brim. Career wise he was doing well, intellectually vigorous, his work came easily. Physically, he was fit and never more aware of it. Emotionally he was in uncharted waters.

Having a break from the office had restored his sense of balance, although he couldn't stifle the rise of excitement he felt as he neared the end of Palmer Street. In a few minutes he would be seeing her for the first time in six days. Six days!

A few straight answers were what he needed from Ashley and he had every intention of getting them.

'Ashley,' he said, striding briskly into his office. 'Bring in my diary, please. We've got to shuffle some things around!' She was packing up for the day, but made no quibble about unpacking. Briefly outlining what he wanted altered they settled into the business of re-scheduling priorities.

'Can you give me an hour or so now?' he

asked when that job was done. He was busily scribbling another series of notes on a pad.

'Yes, of course,' she replied thinking he wanted her to work later still.

'Then let's go somewhere for an early dinner.' He saw her look of surprise and added, 'Please!'

'Why is it necessary to trick me into it,' she asked coldly.

'Why not, nothing else has worked!' he replied, matching her tone.

'Why must we go out to dinner together?' there was annoyance in her voice, but also something else which told him she was defensive.

'Because there are some matters, I want to discuss with you privately, away from this place. I am also tired and hungry.' He stated this baldly, looking her straight in the eye. Something changed in her expression, a stirring of interest.

'Well!' he demanded, when no immediate reply was forthcoming.

'Where do you suggest we go,' she had capitulated.

Fifteen minutes later they were at Ziggy's, being ushered to a quiet table screened by a potted palm. This time they were the first customers to arrive, not the last. Asked for her preference in drinks, she indicated for him to choose. Brian, who felt he could do with the boost from a big full-bodied red wine, instead chose the lighter Merlot thinking it would suit her better.

She looked nervously expectant as Ziggy fussed around making a great production of pouring the wine. Seeing her withdraw her notebook from her handbag Brian told her to put it away. He wasted no time on chit chat, she was off balance and he wanted to press the advantage.

'I want to know what happened between you and Helen on the day you started working for the firm,' he began without preamble.

'Helen would have told you exactly what happened,' she looked at him openly. 'I took advantage of the situation,' she said, making no attempt to justify her action. This was the girl he thought vulnerable! He let her continue without interruption as she recounted the events of that memorable afternoon.

'Do you often do that sort of thing?' he asked when she finished.

'No! Never! It was entirely instinctive! Fateful, if you like, rather exciting,' she smiled fleetingly, looking at him waiting for his reaction.

'What would you have done if it wasn't your type of job?' he asked, bemused by the boldness of his lovely, delicate looking secretary.

'Excused myself and departed,' she replied. 'As I would have done had you been fat and ugly!' The small inferred compliment brought a lick of excitement. She appeared guileless, but Brian wondered if she was teasing.

'So! I'm not fat and ugly!' said the prosecutor, side-tracked for the moment.

'No!' she said it softly, with a hint of a smile, perhaps she was teasing.

'How do I appear to you,' he could feel his concentration drifting as he fished for another compliment.

'Very nice,' she replied, not looking up from her glass of wine.

Ziggy appeared at their table with the menu and to describe their various speciality dishes. For someone who was supposed to be hungry, Brian displayed little interest in what was on offer, choosing something Ziggy suggested would go well with the wine they were drinking. Ashley went along with the same suggestion.

'If I'm nice, why did you let me into your life, then freeze me out of it?' he demanded quietly as soon as Ziggy was gone. Back on track and getting to the core issue.

'Because it's not appropriate,' she replied just as firmly.

'Why?' he demanded again, this time louder, 'because we work together?' He continued without waiting for an answer. 'Ashley, there is something between us, I am sure of it. That day in your apartment, I thought it unmistakable. Surely, we can explore what we have with enough discretion to avoid gossip,' he argued passionately.

'I am deeply sorry for what I have done,' she began earnestly. 'I shouldn't have accepted your help, or kissed you as I did, it gave you the wrong idea.' Now her eyes were shadowy with distress. 'There is an impediment Brian, and until it is resolved we can only be colleagues.'

'What sort of impediment!' he was stunned. He couldn't imagine what Ashley meant.

'If you remember where we first met you will understand,' she told him quietly. 'It is for your benefit not mine,' there was no doubt she meant what she said.

'You were adamant we haven't met before!' he accused sharply. 'I've got no idea where I first saw you. I'm thinking I imagined it,' he was getting agitated. Ashley had him tied up in knots. She constantly hurt his feelings, yet still he wanted her, badly, and now a riddle. Temper sparked inside him. He kept it on a tight leash, but it flared in his eyes and she saw it.

'I understand your frustration, I really do and again I am sorry,' her voice tailed off. Ziggy chose this particular moment to serve dinner.

They began eating Ziggy's appetising and aromatic sautéed veal medallions with balsamic braised tomatoes, roast parsnips and potatoes without noticing what was on their plates. Eventually Brian gave up on the food, gave up the flash of anger.

'How long have I got to remember this so called 'impediment', he queried.

'One week,' Ashley replied, surprising in herself the knowledge she too wanted the matter settled without further delay. He argued for enlightenment here and now but Ashley wouldn't be moved.

'One week,' she repeated, 'that is the deadline.' They sat in silence for a time, fiddling with their glasses of wine.

'Who is Chris?' Brian asked abruptly, he had to know.

'My doctor,' replied a startled Ashley. As undisguised shock spread across Brian's features, Ashley realised the breadth of his misconception.

'Christine Forrest is my doctor,' Ashley gently stressed, 'and she is buying an apartment in Light House. Stella Gollo is buying one too and we all went out to dinner together to celebrate.'

There was nothing more to say. Brian paid the bill and they left the restaurant. It wasn't far to the car, or to Ashley's apartment, very soon their time together would be over.

'Ashley!' he reached out and grasped her arm pulling her around to face him. 'I apologise for my clumsy remarks. I just want this difficulty between us resolved.' Relief washed over him as he saw the tautness in her face ease.

'If we are two of a kind it should be easy,' was her puzzling reply.

In an effort to lighten the conversation she mentioned her old boss Forbes Williams and his wife Anna would be in town in soon. It would be a good opportunity to have a house warming party and for them to meet her new acquaintances.

'I would like to ask Helen,' she said, as they walked up the steps to Light House.

'Helen has almost endowed you with supernatural powers,' Brian replied, trying to be lighter too, 'when she sees the Angels she'll freak out!'

'My artefacts,' Ashley was amused!

'How are your 'artefacts' anyway,' Brian queried, 'I've often thought of them.'

'Perhaps you can see for yourself,' she replied, 'next week.'

'Next week,' he repeated quietly, watching as she located her keys in her handbag and fitted one into the lock of the door to Light House.

A little curl by her ear came loose, he touched it gently. She looked up on the instant and saw the longing deeply etched on his face. She immediately looked away but not before he had seen her reaction. His finger travelled lightly down her jaw line to her chin and then pressed more firmly, to turn her face toward him.

'It would seem I am not the only one with the wrong idea,' he tried to tease, his eyes giving the lie. She turned her head away, just as persistently he turned it back.

'Help me, Ashley,' he whispered, but Ashley remained immobile and mute.

'Please,' he asked softly, tilting her face up so that she had to look at him. In the fading light he saw a flicker of consent and waited no longer. So long desired, so long denied, the kiss, once allowed, completely swept them away. Dim awareness of her touch deepened the embrace. Both totally consumed, for as long as the night took to absorb the remainder of the dusk, they clung to each other, separating in the dark.

'Now tell me if I have the wrong idea?' he whispered unevenly against her cheek.

'One week,' she whispered back, pressing her hands against his chest. He could feel her trembling, knew she was upset.

'Ashley?' he released his hold, trying to pull himself together, trying to see her face.

'One week,' she repeated, slipping quickly through the door shutting it firmly on him. Full of her fragrance, her taste, her feel, he stood staring at the big black door of Light House. Several minutes passed before he moved away.

He didn't remember returning to his car, but the big black door of Light House loomed large in Brian's mind as he started to drive off down Palmer Street. It compelled him to stop. Something was stirring. Something about Light House!

'I'm getting to the bottom of this,' he muttered aloud to himself, 'if I have to drive up and down Palmer Street all night!' The words were the trigger. It came back in its entirety. Stunned for several minutes, he sat staring into space as the events of a night ten years ago unfolded in his mind.

Excitement gripped him somewhere in the middle. Thrusting the car into gear he swung it around and drove back, stopping in the same place as ten years ago. The streetscape was the same! He couldn't believe it! The old red brick building with the 'For Sale' sign on it and sandwiched between two recently erected modern office blocks!

He scrambled out of the car, raced across the road, up the steps and pounded on the big black door.

CHAPTER 6
The Choosing

His urgent summons gained him swift entry into Light House. Inside he was blind to everything except Ashley, who had come out of her apartment to meet him at the top of the stairs. The classic beauty of the place had been restored, but he only saw her at its centre.

She had changed into a long dark house gown and loosened her hair. Rich red-gold and wildly curly, it framed her face like an aura. Her unaltered appearance from that night long ago drew a gasp of astonishment.

'Brian!' she softly called as he took the stairs two at a time, 'what are you doing here?' Thick carpet muffled his footsteps, emphasising the emptiness of the building, emphasising her solitude! Up close he saw her dress was dark smoky blue, like her eyes, where awareness of their embrace still smouldered!

'I met you opposite this building very late one night about ten years ago!' He spoke gruffly, ignoring her question. 'Is that what this is all about?'

'Yes,' she replied.

'You looked exactly as you do now!'

'You do too,' there was a small silence.

'Why couldn't you have reminded me of the incident!' he wanted to know.

'Because it was no ordinary incident,' she was speaking quietly but with slight unevenness. Taking a deep breath, she said, 'I believe we shared a unique psychic experience. It wasn't something I could mention, you would have thought me mad.'

He stared at her in disbelief.

'Are you saying I imagined it after all!' he exclaimed loudly. 'I know I saw you! You disappeared almost in front of my eyes,' his voice trailed off. He had come full circle.

'Think about it, Brian,' Ashley interposed, 'ten years ago I was a sixteen-year-old school girl living in Sydney. I had short cropped hair and wore braces on my teeth. I had an amazing dream where a handsome man came to my assistance and I had a few words of conversation with him,' she let that sink in.

'What were you really like in those days?' she asked.

'Thinner! Longish hair! It was the fashion! Not at all handsome,' he was incredulous. 'Do you really believe we saw into the future,' his spirits rose. Against all his training and his practical common sense, he embraced the concept of a psychic encounter with Ashley.

'The fact I am here proves it,' she said.

'How?' he was fascinated.

'I followed my dream! It brought me to this place, then on the same day, to you,' Ashley replied.

'Why so long? Why did you wait so long?' the question was plaintive and not fair or reasonable, but he was thinking only of the fact they had lost ten years.

'I was half educated and untrained,' she said sensibly. 'You wouldn't have looked at me. I doubt we would have met. Besides, I had obligations to those I loved. I came when I was free.' Ashley could see Brian mentally digesting the information given him and sorting out a string of questions.

Following her into the apartment he noticed her private lobby was filled with greenery, a welcome relief from the weight of Victoriana outside. The apartment had an odd charm, attractive, but not altogether serene, as if there was some underlying discord. She has put the Angels to work he observed, and for some unknown reason the thought pleased him. They no longer dominated the room but were pushed back against the long side wall, well separated, providing space between for dining furniture.

In the overall square of the apartment, the kitchen and bathroom together took out a rectangular bite, leaving an alcove on either side. One side was the entry proper, the other Ashley's bedroom. From the living area you could see a little of the foot of her bed. To shield it from view it had been placed back-to-back with a massive carved wardrobe. He was intrigued to see she slept in a romantic four poster bed, complete with misty white curtains. No sign of the little single bed now.

Ashley's tension was obvious as they seated themselves on the settee in front of the gas-fire the flames set low, more for the appearance of comfort than the need of heat.

'Have you ever had a similar experience?' she seemed almost afraid to ask.

'No! Nothing remotely like it!' he replied quickly and was dismayed to see she was upset by his negative response. 'Why is it so important?'

'I often dream, just like the one we shared,' she explained so softly he had to strain to hear, 'but you are the only one who ever 'saw' me. I hoped you were a 'dreamer' too.'

Deep disappointment darkened her eyes and he would have given anything to take back his reply.

'I always intended finding you,' she said determined to continue, 'I knew we 'met' in

Palmer Street, I saw the street name. I guessed it was in Adelaide because I was born here. It is the only place I had any connection with except for where I was brought up and lived. The rest was instinct and intuition. You recognised me, and I was waiting for you to bring me into your confidence. When it didn't happen, I grew impatient and invited you to Light House, that didn't work either. All it did was fuel the infatuation between us.'

'Infatuation!' Brian exclaimed, stung to the core and rising to his feet. 'I am in love with you!' He lowered his voice a little, 'and you love me! You know it and I know it. Everybody knows it!' he was pacing a little.

'Everybody?' she asked faintly.

'Charles putting up with me working at Henderson's is a clear sign he's giving me a warning to resolve my personal affairs,' he replied sharply. 'If Charles knows then the whole firm is full of it!' If he was making a fool of himself, he didn't care.

'We are in love,' he told her emphatically, pulling her up to face him, standing close. 'Why describe what we feel as infatuation when you know it is so much more?' his eyes compelled an answer.

'Because I have come to believe I am not normal,' she said sadly. She hushed his protests with a gentle gesture. 'Dreaming has taken over my life; a disturbance while I am sleeping is terrifying. It's as if my body needs me and I am unable to get back. I am afraid of being trapped in a ghostly half world. I came looking for your help. I found Light House instead and a measure of peace.' Brian would have interrupted again but she put a gentle finger to his lips, sealing them.

'I thought this old building significant because it marked the starting point of my search for you. Instead, it has provided respite. Living here I am in control and there seems to be a future unfolding. I think it must be what I was meant to find.'

There was absolute stillness in the room. An uncanny feeling the Angels were listening prickled Brian's senses. Even the huge carved wardrobe, standing like the guardian of her bed chamber, seemed an eavesdropper. He dismissed the fantasy, concentrating on her soft voice.

'I love you too,' she said simply and her words fell on his ears with indescribable sweetness. 'I want to be with you,' she said, 'I would be if you were a Dreamer, but you are not and I am afraid to take that step.'

Barely breathing her name, he whispered, 'you foolish, foolish girl.' Barricading yourself in this place isn't the answer,' he was thinking of the doors barring the way into her apartment. 'You need someone to look after you. Some treatment! Some advice'!

'I've had treatment and advice! Loads of it! From the time I was little,' Ashley replied, moving away from him.

'They all said I would grow out of it and so I did for a time. It came back when I was about fifteen. I found it exciting and kept it secret. It was easy because by that time I was living with Forbes and Anna Williams and free, in a limited way, to do as I pleased. It became a normal part of my life for years. Then circumstances changed. My solitude ended. I was subjected to frequent disturbance and the frightening experiences began.' Brian could see it was difficult for Ashley to speak openly. 'I am not normal,' she said sadly. 'I do not wish to hurt you, but I cannot see a future for us.'

'You are forgetting the way we met,' replied Brian quietly. 'It appears to me I have potential.' This time he didn't allow interruption.

'If our dream was a guide to your future, why not mine too? Why was I so easy for you to find and on the same day, no less! I think Light House the 'marker'. We are meant for each other!'

Ashley shook her head solemnly, 'I think you were the enticement,' she was gravely sure of herself. 'Light House is more than it appears and I am caught up in it!' Ashley was standing in front of the gas fire and for the first time Brian noticed the seascape that hung over the fireplace. It's simple beach scene, charmingly familiar and in stark contrast to the brooding strangeness of the room, seemed to frame Ashley. It seemed touchingly significant.

'Remember I told you Light House originally housed an unorthodox religious sect known as the 'Sisters of Light'. They were spiritual healers and had a strong following of women here in Adelaide around 1860 to 1870. Christine Forrest is taking an apartment soon and so too is Fay Bennett, Ernest's friend. Fay is a counsellor and plans to work from Light House utilising a room or two on the ground floor. It was Christine's suggestion. It is strange the building is reverting to something after the style of its original purpose.'

'What has that got to do with your 'dreaming' problem?' Brian wanted to know.

'Nothing really, except I feel it is right and I could be involved some way in the development of Light House,' Ashley answered honestly.

'Does Christine Forrest have anything to say about your problem?'

'It's not her field, but we have discussed it,' Ashley replied. 'She suggests it may be a self-imposed delusion. I don't agree, but I can't expect her to understand.'

Privately Brian was inclined to agree with Christine, but wisely kept his own counsel.

'Why were you living with Forbes Williams,' he asked, after all Forbes was her old boss, 'and what changed your circumstances?'

'I lived with Forbes and Anna from the time I started at St. Anne's College. My guardians, Uncle Max and Aunt Ellen, enrolled me as a boarder, then worried should my 'dreaming' return I would not be treated appropriately. I sometimes have symptoms of a heart attack, chest pains, difficulty breathing. I am best left to fight through it alone. Forbes, who was their legal advisor and friend, offered accommodation in his house.'

'What happened to your parents?' Brian asked sympathetically.

'They both died in a car accident when I was about six months old, I nearly died too,' she replied matter-of-factly. It was an old sad story told to her years ago.

'My parents were travelling from Adelaide to Glenbourne, south of Sydney, to join Max and Ellen in business when their car was hit by another vehicle. Aunt Ellen always believed the accident was responsible for my sleep disorder.'

'I'm sorry,' said Brian.

'I was sorry for Aunt and Uncle, when I was old enough to understand. They were in their mid-sixties and planning retirement, when they became parents. They gave up their plans and continued in their businesses, believing it was their duty to raise the last remaining Preston. Aunt Ellen's haberdashery shop became a crèche. She was an unlikely mother, but an efficient one and always ready to take advice from her customers. In fact, she told me it, improved business.

Max took it upon himself to clothe me, and then paraded me along Main Street, between their shops. All the Preston men, Grandfather, Uncle Max and my father were tailors. I had properly tailored clothes before I could walk. My childhood was happy, perhaps unusual, because I was more a fiercely protected toy than a child. They discouraged me mixing with other children, but I didn't mind because

I didn't really know how to socialise. Other children treated me as an oddity because of my old parents and strange clothes. My circumstances changed when Uncle Max died nearly two years ago and I went home to look after Aunt Ellen.' Ashley moved back to the settee; Brian remained standing by the mantelpiece.

'In Forbes' house,' she continued, 'I had my own room upstairs. After dinner each night Forbes would retire to his study, Anna to her own sitting room, and I to mine. They were both totally absorbed in their professions. Anna paints and spends most days in her studio; evenings are reserved for dealing with any business matters arising from her work or from the running of her household.

Each day Forbes would drive me to college and have me picked up at the end of the school day. Friday afternoon, I would be driven to the train station to be sent back to Glenbourne, for the weekend. Max would be waiting at the other end. On Monday morning the routine would be reversed. Life was so regimented I welcomed my dreaming when it returned. It was so vividly exciting, I became obsessed. My routine remained the same even when I worked for Forbes.

When Max died, I shifted back to Glenbourne to become Aunt Ellen's carer. She was in her late eighties, desperately lost without Max and in rapidly failing health. Her deteriorating condition meant she called on me any time. Night time disturbances affected me so badly I was afraid of sleeping.

One morning after a better night than usual, I brought in her breakfast tray. She thanked me and said 'Max and I adored you. You brought us immense joy'. Later when I came back for her tray, I found her in the same position, smiling peacefully, breakfast untouched. She had passed away.'

Ashley paused for a little while, staring down at her hands clasped in her lap.

'It didn't mark the end of my bad dreams though,' she continued, 'I had to finalise her estate, dismantle her home and dispose of some of her possessions. It broke my heart.

My dreams were morbid and gloomy and I was afraid of being alone.

I moved to Adelaide to find you, but you didn't recognise me as a kindred spirit. I disliked living in a hotel; there were too many people around, much like my dreams only real. Light House brought peace.'

Listening to Ashley, Brian formed the opinion she was simply the product of her upbringing. Her attraction to Light House was understandable, since it represented the security of Forbes' house all over again. Light House's magnetism, he rationalised was driven by emotional need.

Hearing her story unfold, he marvelled at the mystery he had endowed upon her. A hungry heart is a powerful force, he mused, and it plays tricks on the mind. Being with her, secluded in dimly lit luxury, was a balm to his spirit. The faint sense of discord noticed earlier had vanished. Now the apartment seemed overwhelmingly romantic. Shadows, subtly sensual, moved around the room. The curtains of the four-poster bed stirred. She loved him, and hearing her say it was an exquisite thrill.

'I live half a life,' she was saying, 'I was hoping for a full one but now doubt it is possible. When I leave work, I am reclaimed by this place. I have come to believe there is a purpose, and whatever it is will hurt you. That is why we cannot be together.'

It was a cold shock. Whatever influences abound under this old roof, real or imagined, they were affecting Ashley, she was the one in danger. A sensitive and imaginative girl kept hostage by a strong sense of duty, left too long in seclusion and suddenly freed, was bound to have difficulty adjusting to normal life.

As Helen considered Ashley mysteriously compelling, so Ashley was bestowing that same endowment upon Light House. Brian respected Ashley's psychic gift, but only to a certain extent.

'You have no right to make such a decision for me!' he said it kindly but with unmistakable firmness. She was so tense his mild admonishment shook her composure. 'And I will not lose you to some premonition!'

She visibly paled; her eyes huge with distress.

'How do you propose we continue,' he asked very gently when it became obvious, she was too emotional to speak easily.

'I will resign, of course,' she replied.

'And what good would that do?' he asked, coming over to her on the couch.

'Love is the most important thing in this world. I thought it wasn't coming to me, but it has, in the most freakish way. Whatever happened that night, ten years ago, it buried itself within me and until a few months ago I was shielded from loneliness. Then from the moment you stepped into my office, my overwhelming desire was and still is, to carry you off. If you meant it when you said you loved me, then I would risk any mortal thing to be with you.' He paused for a few moments and then asked, 'Do you love me Ashley?

Her tears told him all. They poured forth unstoppable, real grief, hard sobs revealing deep worries. Tenderly holding her close, he patiently waited for the pent-up emotion to subside.

'Go powder your nose,' he said after a while, kissing away tears and mopping up her wet face. 'We both need to get out of this place,' he declared. 'Let's go somewhere for coffee.' Ashley offered to make the coffee but Brian was firm in his refusal.

'Don't you like Light House?' Ashley queried rather forlornly.

'There is an atmosphere here that confuses me. You admitted Light House is more than it seems. My advice to you would be to move out as soon as possible. Let me have a look at your lease, I may be able to get you out of it,' was his forthright reply.

'It isn't as simple as that,' she replied. 'Light House is mine. I own it!' It was the last thing Brian expected to hear.

'You do?' He was incredulous, 'how?'

'Inheritance and insurance,' Ashley replied tiredly, 'it is the other reason apart from dreaming that makes me think I am different.' She looked at Brian bravely, like one about to confess a guilty secret.

'My Grandparents died shortly after I was

born. Grandfather suffered a heart attack and Grandmother a few weeks later of pneumonia. My father Maurice was an only child and inherited both estates. Our family is small, Uncle Max and Aunt Ellen our only blood relatives. They came to Adelaide for both funerals and then to my Christening. It was at this last event Max suggested Maurice relocate our family to Glenbourne. Maurice could join Max in business and Angelina, my mother, could join Aunt Ellen in her shop. As I have told you they were killed in an accident only a few kilometres from Glenbourne. My parent's estates came to me with Uncle Max named as guardian. He enlisted Forbes Williams to sue for compensation on my behalf, and Forbes won me a huge claim. Forbes set up the 'Angels Trust' and he and Max in collaboration invested my money. I actually own his Chambers. That came about when he wanted to buy a waterfront property on the Harbour. My living in his house was probably part of the deal. To my knowledge the Trust has never been drawn on for any expenses.

Max and Ellen's estates were being wound up when I saw the Angels. I was so taken with them I phoned Forbes. His agents checked out the property and now it belongs to the 'Angel's Trust', of which I am the sole beneficiary.'

Considerably surprised by the revelation, the fact remained, Brian's opinion of Light House was unchanged.

'You seem to be suggesting destiny is linking you to Light House. It is all too circumstantial. You are not responsible for your parent's accident and it's not your fault you are the last of a small family. Surely, you've been in our profession long enough to know there are many strange stories connected with wills and trusts.

As for Light House, you were fortunate enough to have enough collateral to indulge your fantasy. Some of the best business decisions have been made on a hunch, in time I think this will prove a good one. Never-the-less, I still think you need to get away from the place,' he said determinedly and hurried her into collecting her jacket.

His comment was a breath of fresh air and added to the sense of release as they made their way outside into the cool darkness of the night. Like a picture drawn of the past, they stepped directly into the scene of their 'meeting' so long ago and were both newly amazed.

'I was lonely and wishing for someone that night,' Brian confessed. 'How strange you appeared here in front of Light House.'

'You saw a danger and rescued me,' Ashley replied. New understanding was dawning as she gazed intensely into his face.

'I saw you for much longer than a few seconds,' she admitted. 'I was with you in your car and in your house. I thought you sensed my presence. Did you?'

'Yes, and there was a fragrance. It is the one you are wearing tonight. Ashley, what are you telling me?'

'Would you take me as I am and Light House too?

'You know I would,' he said simply.

'Then I would like to complete our journey,

the one we started ten years ago.'

'I may not bring you back!' he warned.

'We will be back,' she said seriously, waiting for him to open the car door. 'But you must be very sure!

He took her face between his hands, kissing her long and deep. He was very sure.

CHAPTER 7
The Bay

Brian couldn't sleep. His mind was too busy turning over the events of the past twenty-four hours. Fearing movement might disturb her, he lay very still. Relaxed in his arms, breathing gently on his chest, she seemed to be at peace, but he worried she was dreaming.

A sublime magic, different from anything he had ever experienced suffused his body, leaving him weak. Ashley did that to him. She could take away his strength and then give it back tenfold. He nuzzled her brow, kissing her lightly as an angel's touch.

They were lovers. That was the greatest miracle. He thought, hoped, he had been gentle.

Impatient for love, but unused to it, she had startled at his every touch. Tender whisperings put her at ease, allowing for a sweet discovery of each other. For a few desperate moments her curiosity nearly brought about his undoing, he becoming the led, instead of leader. After that, there was no holding back. They clung together fiercely wanting to be part of each other, to be full, sated, complete. Eventually they were.

Little had been said on the journey to his house. Her quickened interest on nearing their destination completely stifled conversation. Very little had been said when they arrived, both struck with silence.

Profoundly curious about her reaction to his home he ushered Ashley into his living room calmly enough, standing with her while she took in her surroundings.

In complete contrast to Light House, his big solid bungalow sprawled comfortably in a leafy garden. Inside it was light, spacious and sparsely furnished, owning neither mood, nor mystery. For the first time he saw his home as it would appear to others, as bare as a blank canvas.

At his invitation, Ashley wandered about while he attempted to make coffee. It was difficult to concentrate; he couldn't remember where he kept anything. His eyes, with a will of their own, followed her around the living room. Her fingers touching the back of his armchair, lightly touching his books, seemed to trail along his nerve ends. She moved beyond the living room out of sight and he began on the coffee again, dropping everything at the sound of her voice. He found her in his bedroom.

'I remember seeing you here,' she had whispered

'This part of the house is unchanged,' he began nervously. It was on his mind to tell her it was the house he lived in with Mike, then alone after Mike moved on. That he bought the place when it came up for sale, gradually altering it over the years. It didn't seem relevant.

'Are you unchanged from my dream?' she had asked, lightly touching the buttons of his shirt. Her message seemed clear but he hesitated, gripped by unreasonable panic. Could this possibly be another psychic experience!

'Don't tease me Ashley,' his voice a rough whisper.

'I'm not,' she had whispered back, running her fingers up to his collar, drawing him to her, 'I'm inviting.'

Looking into her lovely face, irrationality dissolved, along with hesitation. Each had travelled an unlikely path to this moment, now they were arrived.

Ashley stirred, breaking his reverie. She stretched fully, causing upheaval among the blankets.

'Are you all right?' he whispered, needing to know.

'Yes,' she softly replied.

'Ashley, were you dreaming?' he whispered, as she snuggled against his warm, accommodating body.

'Yes,' she whispered back, 'about you. You were making love to me.'

'So I was,' he murmured, caught up in that tide again, caring for only one thing in the onrush. That he took her with him.

It was closer to lunch than breakfast

time before they surfaced, Brian first to wake, sliding out of bed carefully so as not to disturb her. Twenty minutes later he emerged from his bathroom, showered, shaved and casually dressed in jeans and sweater. Picking up various pieces of clothing lying on the floor, he put his own away and neatly placed Ashley's things on a chair.

'What are you doing with that?' a sweet clear voice enquired. Caught red handed admiring her little silk teddy, he blushed to the roots of his hair.

'Picking up your stuff,' he grinned, 'there's not much of it.' He came to her on the bed, smothering her with kisses. They were unrestrainedly, unselfconsciously, irrepressibly happy.

Ashley showered and dressed while Brian prepared an ambrosial breakfast of leathery omelettes, cold toast and excellent, hot, strong coffee. He phoned Charles and then Helen. The day was their own, the week-end too.

Sunny skies greeted them when they stepped outside. A sparkle in the air reflected on the pool and Ashley wanted to swim.

'It's too cold just yet,' Brian explained, 'I'll take you somewhere warmer.'

'Where,' she asked curiously?

'Rocky Bay, our family have a house there. I helped Dad build it when I was a lad. The house is basic, the Bay is nice and there is a rock pool deep enough for a swim. It is usually a couple of degrees warmer than the sea.'

For weeks Brian had been hankering to visit the coast, now the opportunity presented itself he couldn't wait to get going.

'We'll need a few provisions,' he said ransacking his cupboards, 'no one uses the place over winter so no food is there, and shops are non-existent.' Ashley looked into the box he was packing. Wine, steak, bread and potatoes, she noted and phoned Stella Gollo.

They arrived back at Light House in a breathless rush, sunlight following them into its dim foyer. Upstairs Ashley collected two paper bags from her wooden box on the hall table and handed them to Brian while she unlocked the door.

'What's this?' he asked.

'My breakfast and lunch,' she replied, 'Maria delivers it. It may come in handy.' Brian thought it amusing she didn't bother to make herself toast or cut a sandwich.

He followed her inside. In daylight, sunshine from tall windows dispelled shadows and gloom, the lobby seemed greener, the apartment brighter. Last night's confusing atmosphere was gone, in its place romantic luxury. He wandered around taking another look, stopping in front of the seascape. It was like scores of beach scenes, in a vague way even resembling Rocky Bay. He noticed the artist's signature.

'Did Anna Williams paint this?' he asked, turning around, expecting Ashley still to be packing an overnight bag.

'Yes, it was a gift from her when I left Sydney,' she replied, 'I asked her to paint a scene for me,' she looked up and stopped. Brian was staring at her. In the process of changing clothes, she was ready to step into her jeans and was only wearing bra and tiny knickers.

The expression on his face was unmistakable and entirely predictable for a new lover. She was secretly delighted, at the same time alarmed.

'No! Not here, Brian! Not ever in this place!'

'I haven't said a word,' he protested, crossing the room with obvious amorous intent.

'You didn't need to!' she smiled at him but her eyes were serious.

'You parade around in next to nothing beside the most inviting bed I've ever seen and tell me 'not here, ever!' Come one Ashley, be fair!' He was half joking, half serious.

'I have a strong premonition about it. It is something you will have to get used to!' she said, pulling on her jeans with determination. 'I want to make love too, but not here! It will be better when we reach Rocky Bay.'

'That's more than two hours away!' he complained.

'Then best we get moving,' she replied.

Stella Gollo was waiting for them downstairs with a large hamper. Her bright brown eyes missed nothing. If a man makes you look like that, Stella decided, he is the right one.

'What's this?' Brian asked for the second time that afternoon, after introductions were made.

'Ashley asked for a hamper,' Stella replied, handing it to him. 'This should last two or three days, plenty of good food and champagne.'

She waved them goodbye from the pavement. It was a bright new day for all three, last night Stella had slept in her new apartment for the first time.

Freedom gave them wings. The outskirts of the city rapidly disappeared in a diminishing trail of houses and shops. Flying along the open road, hood down, wind in their faces the little car skimmed dips and rises, slowing down through townships, taking off again at first chance. Branching off the highway onto a dirt road made rough from winter weather, slowed down their journey. Picking his way carefully past ruts and washaways, Brian stopped at the crest of a hill.

'There it is,' he said, 'Rocky Bay, well, if unimaginatively named.'

Two outcrops of large granite boulders tumbled down to the sea, cupping between them a small sandy beach. A few wispy tamarisk trees cast fragile shadows around two small, wooden holiday houses, weathered grey like the rocks.

'Which is your house?' asked Ashley, her face shining in anticipation.

'Neither,' he replied, 'ours is almost directly beneath us. You can't see it from here.' Driving off again they were soon approaching his place, nestled at the bottom of the hill.

Ashley loved the little house, which looked much like the other two, the only difference being an upstairs room.

At beach level the bay seemed bigger. She loved the warm sand and strong, uncompromising rocks. She loved the sound of surging waves dumping on the beach. She loved the clatter of upended pebbles tumbling over each other, growing smooth in the process of chasing the retreating waves back to their place on the seabed. She loved the salty, sea-weedy smell.

Unlocking the house, turning on the electricity, unpacking the car, took a few minutes then they were out on the beach, eager to be part of it all.

'Where is the rock pool?' she asked, excited as a child.

They splashed through the shallows to a cluster of rocks at the end of the bay. Brian climbed among them, Ashley close, at his heels, until he stopped and drew her forward. They stood on a natural shelf of rock, with the pool lapping at their feet.

'It's absolutely beautiful!' Ashley gasped, taking in the rugged surrounds that held back a booming sea.

'Swimming here and from the beach can be dangerous. Fishing is poor too. So, you can understand why it isn't popular. That's our good luck. We always have the place to ourselves.'

'What about the other two houses?' asked Ashley.

'Never have we seen them occupied.'

She looked at him and smiled. Here they were in a place gloriously warm, the ledge and surrounds a natural sun trap, clear blue water, azure sky and complete seclusion.

'I'm going in,' she said pulling off her sweater, stepping out of her jeans and underclothes. Plunging neatly into the pool, surfacing with barely a splash, she laughed aloud in sheer delight.

It was a revelation, watching her swim. He fumbled with his own clothes as she darted up and down the length of the pool, inspecting the bottom, appearing here and there then diving out of sight, like a water sprite.

He went in after her, splashing around. Surfacing in front of him he tried to catch her but she was too quick, too slippery. Cavorting around in the pool, a long narrow entrapment of water at the base of the bluff, squeals of delight and shouts of deeper laughter echoed around the rocks. She eluded him with ease until ready to be caught, and then made no effort to wriggle away. They sunk to the bottom of the pool coiled together, rising fast to the surface for air.

In the last heat of the afternoon, they made love urgently and awkwardly, on the ledge, using their discarded clothing for bedding, later resting against each other, taking comfort in the softness of human flesh.

Wandering home, in the fading light of day, carrying their sodden clothing, they were nudists, drunk with love. Much later still, full of Stella's food and champagne, they slept like babies in the little upstairs room, windows open wide to Rocky Bay and the contented, indulgent, sigh of the ocean.

'The rocks are pink!' she whispered, raised on her elbow and gazing out of the window. Dawn's early light heralded another fine day.

'So are you,' he whispered back. Palest pink accentuated her colouring, adding a pearl like lustre to her skin. Eyes, luminous with remembrance of deep pleasure, smiled down at him, melting the marrow of his bones.

'I always brought my treasures to this room,' he murmured.

'Am I one?' she asked.

'You are all,' he replied, kissing the point of her shoulder.

They drifted outside into the pale pink light, examining everything, turning over rocks, looking deep into little pools and seeing nothing except each other's delight. The day became days, each a progression of light to dark and they were only barely aware of the change. Talking for hours, cushioned by warm sand and remembering no specific conversation, their knowledge of each other grew. Swimming in the pool, splashing in shallows or luxuriating on the ledge they were abandoned to the primeval compulsion of sea, sex and sunshine. Braving the ocean and being tugged by an ambush of lurking currents. Forgetting hunger and thirst until Stella's hamper reminded them of another appetite.

At night in the dark, the sea and the shore continued their unending discourse. Respectfully left in peace, the two little houses maintained their mystery. A fire burning brightly in their house signalled to the world all within was snug and content. They wanted to stay forever, delaying their departure for as long as possible.

Journeying home quietly through a night of black velvet spangled with tiny stars, slowly on the rough uneven road, swiftly along the highway, carefully through towns, finally coming to a reluctant halt in Brian's garage.

Unlocking the door into his house, he scooped Ashley up and carried her over the threshold. Down the hallway, past the telephone with its flashing message light, falling onto his bed, both laughing, her arms tightly clasped around his neck.

'All the way home I've been thinking Rocky Bay is paradise and how soon can we return,' he paused for breath, 'then I realised something absolutely wonderful.'

'What?' she asked, inelegantly, trying to bite his ear.

'Paradise is being with you!'

CHAPTER 8
The Party

Looking pretty resting against her pillows, Ashley smiled lazily at Brian as he approached. Smartly dressed and ready for work he was thinking of the day ahead.

'Are you absolutely sure about this?' he asked, his clothing make small rustling sounds as he sat on the edge of their bed. Ashley refused to continue as his secretary and no amount of discussion would change her mind.

'Just look at me Brian,' she replied, 'surely you can see it would be wrong.'

'Dressed like that, I agree,' he smiled, admiring her wisp of night-dress.

'I wasn't talking about clothes,' she chided.

'I know,' he said softly. She looked like a woman very much loved. Office staff would pick up on it instantly. If she was sensitive about such matters, perhaps it was better to resign. The fact that she didn't want to go back to Light House straight away was encouraging.

They planned she should return there late afternoon to gather up a few things. He would prefer to go back there with her, but could afford no more time off. At least during daylight hours Ashley would have company. Kissing her one last time, promising to pick her up no later than seven p.m., he left.

Feeling lonely after the intense intimacy of the past three days, Ashley couldn't settle. Wandering around Brian's empty house, suddenly swimming seemed a good idea. Dressed only in her nightdress with her long white beach coat doubling as a dressing gown, Ashley stepped into the greyness of early morning. Winter was back, sharpening up the chill. Ignoring weather and the pool's dark stare Ashley slipped out of her garments and dived in without hesitation.

Frigid water laid in wait like an assassin and sucked away her breath. Gasping for air, arms powerless, legs heavy and unresponsive, she struggled for movement. Somehow, she managed to drag herself up the steps of the pool collapsing onto the tiled surrounds. Pain gripped her chest.

Instinctively knowing to seek warmth she forced her limbs to move. Half standing, she made it inside to the bathroom, collapsing again this time into the bath tub. Numb fingers fumbled with stubborn taps and then gradually hot water began soaking away shock, easing the pressure on her chest, allowing her to breathe. Half dried, clad in Brian's pyjamas the nearest thing to hand, she huddled down into their bed exhausted. After a while she slept soundly, for nearly two hours.

Awake, stretching cautiously, feeling better, she carefully made her way to the kitchen. Toast with honey and some strong coffee helped restore her energy. She phoned Christine Forrest.

Dr. Christine Forrest felt good striding into the medical centre, curiosity stirred by

Ashley's phone call. Because of Ashley an idea was in process of becoming reality, not until viewing the apartments did the possibility of Light House present itself. Christine and colleague Fay Bennett shared a concern for certain patients. More than a few people who used the clinic were trauma victims, seeking medical help outside their own area, to avoid embarrassment. Counselling and advice were sometimes more necessary than medicine. She and Fay could provide such a facility conveniently close to the clinic. Running the idea past her medical colleagues, she found them generally receptive of the idea, provided it didn't impinge on their services.

Fay Bennett was enthusiastic. An independent counsellor, she could please herself where she practised. They instructed their legal advisor to confer with Light House Management to sort out any contractual, lease, or legal difficulties and all was moving along smoothly. Chris was shifting into her new apartment this afternoon.

Dismay replaced curiosity when the

usually impeccably groomed Ashley arrived in rumpled clothing looking completely dishevelled.

'I am worried I may be pregnant,' Ashley confessed bluntly, after briefly explaining she was on her way home after week-end away with Brian.

Although dumbfounded by the news Christine maintained her professional aplomb.

It was she who suggested Ashley needed more social contact. When Ashley later enquired about birth control, Chris presumed a partner had been found. It soon became obvious there was no one in her life except her boss. He seemed unlikely. Calmly assuring Ashley the medication prescribed weeks ago should provide ample protection. Chris gave her a urine test for confirmation.

'The result is negative.' Christine informed a relieved Ashley. Only a slightly bluish tinge around her mouth suggested any other disorder.

'I'll give you a blood test,' Christine added, 'your colour isn't good.'

'It's not necessary,' Ashley replied with such finality it stopped Chris in her tracks. 'I swam in Brian's pool this morning and it was much too cold. I lost my breath. But I am all right now!'

Unused to having her advice dismissed Christine allowed her displeasure to show.

'Come to my apartment around five thirty this afternoon and we will celebrate your arrival at Light House.' Ashley's conciliatory tone smoothed Christine's annoyance. A celebration would be nice she thought, and a chat. She accepted.

Arriving back at Light House Ashley thought of the inconvenience she was causing Helen Gilbertson, so phoned to apologise and extend the same invitation. Helen also accepted.

Charles Briers was in Helen's office at the time of the call, plump with the news Brian had brought him earlier that morning. Disappointed not to be first with the latest, he listened in to the conversation with keen interest.

'Well,' he said with relish when the call ended, 'you've excelled yourself this time!' sarcastically referring to the number of unsuitable secretaries Helen had provided for Brian.

'He's fallen for this one! Hook, line and sinker! I can't believe our bad luck! Fortunately, he's willing to take one of the reserves and has already picked her out! Why couldn't he have done that in the first place! Consult him when he gets back from Henderson's.' Charles was edgy, disliking anything that interfered with the smooth running of the firm.

'Obviously they consider her resignation the most discreet thing to do,' he added, watching for Helen's reaction. 'Disappointed?'

'Yes, but not for the reason you imagine,' Helen replied quickly, aware there were those who suspected she had a crush on Brian. 'Ashley worries me!' Unconvinced, Charles left her office.

Pleased to be putting things right with people she respected Ashley looked to her own appearance. She struggled for a time to bring her own frizzy hair under control but the effort seemed unusually tiring.

Throwing down the comb in exasperation she changed into fresh jeans, white sweater and black blazer and left the building. Brian liked her wild appearance, but even he had suggested a trip to the hairdressers. She would take his advice.

Strolling back some time later, a taxi pulling up in front Light House caught Ashley's eye. An elderly sturdily built man alighted, leaning forward to assist an elegant much smaller woman.

'Forbes! Anna!' she cried out delightedly. 'What a wonderful surprise!' Rushing up and kissing each of them warmly on the cheek, she was too excited to notice their hesitation. Not only were Ashley's looks and style of dress different, the girl they knew would never have kissed them so spontaneously.

'We have come looking for you!' Forbes sounded aggrieved. 'We were worried when you missed your usual phone call. No one knew your whereabouts. Your employer was absent!'

'I am so terribly sorry,' Ashley apologised, 'I went away unexpectedly.'

'We can see you are well,' Anna interrupted soothingly, 'and that is our greatest concern.'

Comfortably settled in Ashley's apartment, pacified with a daintily served morning tea hastily purchased from Maria's Lunch Box, Ashley's guests were ready to converse. Their proposed visit to Adelaide in a week's time was cancelled due to one of Forbes' cases going to trial. He would be extremely busy from now on and wanted to make sure all was well with Ashley before work started. They were returning to Sydney tonight. Scrutinising her expression for any sign of uncertainty, they listened without interruption while Ashley told them about Brian.

'There has been no intimation of friendship,' Forbes remarked, 'so you must agree this relationship has come about suddenly.'

'Do you recall painting that picture, Anna,' Ashley replied indicating the seascape on the wall. 'Do you remember I described the scene and you altered the rock formation because it looked 'too stagey' on canvas?' Anna nodded; Forbes listened patiently. 'Well Brian's family have a little house on a bay very similar to the one I was attempting to describe. We have been there these past few days. I 'saw' Light House and Brian too in a similar way. That is why I came to Adelaide. I didn't know how to explain it to you, so said nothing.'

There were many times over the years Forbes felt uncomfortable with Ashley's solitary life. Max and Ellen had worried about Ashley 'seeing' things in her sleep. Perhaps she did. Forbes dealt in facts. The facts of the matter are that her investment is solid and the young woman radiantly happy.

'When may we meet him?' Forbes asked. 'Could he join us for lunch? We are meeting with Richard Martin, there are things to discuss. Since you have taken Brian Moore into your confidence, it may be useful to have him there too.'

In conference for most of the day at Henderson's, Brian could not be contacted. No messages were passed on. For him the day unfolded in a solid and satisfying manner except he had been unable to contact Ashley. He took comfort from the knowledge she wasn't sitting around in Light House planning to devote her life to that place.

Arriving back at Syms, Simcock at the end of the day ready to discuss matters with Helen, he was surprised to find her gone.

In his rooms Ashley's empty desk stood as a stark reminder of her absence. How he missed her! How absolutely he missed her! Wanting contact, he reached for the phone then saw the little pile of messages. Fanning them out on his desk he saw they covered most of the day. Anxiety flared.

A few minutes later Light House smirked down on him in the gathering dusk. Lights from the closed shops and upstairs windows gave that impression. Urgently buzzing for entry, the big black door offered no resistance so he went inside. Somewhere from within were sounds of muted conversation and laughter. Then Ashley appeared, rosy gold and gorgeous running out of her apartment to greet him. Fear dispelled.

'What's going on?' he asked from inside their ecstatic re-union.

'Forbes and Anna are here!' her voice silvery with excitement.

'Here! Why!' he asked, jolted back into the here and now.

'To meet you, young man!' sounded a voice trained to reach the deepest corners of a court room.

'Forbes Williams,' he stated, introducing himself, 'and you I presume are Brian Robert Harper Moore!' he finished before Brian could speak.

'Yes!' Brian replied, recovering his composure and shaking the proffered hand, 'but I don't use 'Harper', professionally or otherwise. You must have checked me out thoroughly!' His voice carried the tone of inquiry.

'As executor of Ashley's family trust, I have a responsibility. The events of her first twenty-four hours in this city stretched my credibility, so I make no apology for having you investigated.' Forbes statement was unarguable and Brian nodded his agreement'.

'However, it has come up with nothing more ominous than the fact that you choose not to use one of your middle names. Would you mind telling me why?'

'I don't like it!' Brian replied without hesitation, feeling resentful at coming under question but at the same time understanding Forbes' reasons. 'Harper' is my mother's family name. Why are you interested?'

'Aubrey Cyrus Harper was the original owner of Light House!' Forbes replied.

'I believe a distant relative was once reasonably successful here, whether that person was Aubrey Cyrus Harper I do not know. It is not an uncommon name. We may be talking about another family. I can assure you my own family have absolutely no connection with these premises!' Brian found it preposterous to imagine he was connected to Light House.

Forbes remained noncommittal, simply raising another query.

'Ashley tells me you have mixed feelings about this place. Would you enlighten me, please?'

'She was spending too much time alone here. I feared for her health,' Brian replied honestly.

'Well, you appear to have successfully addressed that problem,' Forbes remarked dryly, looking directly at their subject.

'Brian,' Ashley began gently, 'I feel sure you are the connection to this place, not me!' Forbes raised his eyes to the ceiling but said nothing. 'The Angels being here and my family trust being named 'Angels Trust' is simply a coincidence. I feel liberated. Free to choose what to do, not compelled.' she touched his arm.

'Richard Martin has resigned and Forbes suggests I take over his job. I could work from my apartment and be involved with new developments as they arise. It is no more than we would be doing together in our spare time. This way I will be paid for my efforts and have more time to concentrate on our life together. What do you say?'

What could Brian say! His objections were so insubstantial he would be embarrassed to reveal them to Forbes. Besides that, Ashley looked so beautifully earnest, so excited by her vision of the future, it melted away any resistance on his part.

'A building is only a pile of bricks,' he thought to himself while assuring Ashley he would support her in whatever she chose to do.

Joining the party, which had expanded to include everyone connected to Light House, they found Ashley's guests in high good humour. The shopkeepers, elated by an impromptu celebration, greeted Brian like a long-lost friend. Anna immediately impressed with her gentle warmth and grace. Helen, fascinated by the Angels was deep in conversation with Ernest Braithewaite and Richard Martin. Christine Forest's penetrating scrutiny he found rather puzzling. Stella, busy handing around savouries, gave him a conspiratorial grin.

At an appropriate time, Forbes made an amusing speech, welcoming the new tenants, praising the old. Thanking Richard Martin for his services, advising them all Light House now had its own manager who would be available at times to be advised. Ashley was congratulated and with the purpose of the gathering achieved, everyone gradually took their leave.

It was a tight fit getting Forbes into Brian's little car for the trip to the airport, but they managed with good humour and made their flight with minutes to spare.

'Forbes and Anna have unusual stamina for their age,' Brian remarked as they strolled back to his car. 'It has been a long day for them and won't be over for a few more hours!'

'I handed the apartment over to them after lunch,' Ashley replied. 'They had a good long nap while I helped Stella prepare for the party.'

'Why are they allowed to sleep in your bed and not me?' Brian teased, trying to steal a kiss, and being fended off. Her resistance only making him try harder.

'Because my premonition doesn't apply to them,' she explained matter-of-factly.

'Which reminds me, could we call into the apartment on the way home? I have left my night attire by the pool; it is probably damp.'

'How come'? Brian wanted to know and immediately extracted the full story. 'Why did you not mention your breathlessness to Chris! It could have been serious!' Brian was becoming alarmed again.

'It has happened to me before when I have been roughly awoken from a dream. It is nothing to worry about. I have been checked out other times by other doctors. I was fully recovered by the time I arrived at Chris's consulting room, so I asked instead if I was pregnant.'

Shock blurred his thinking. In the heat of passion, he remembered asking Ashley if it was safe. Dismay that there could be an element of deception between them brought pain. Permeating it all a sweet thrill unlike any he had ever known.

'Why did you tell me not to worry?' he asked struggling with this mixture of emotion.

'I didn't want you to stop,' she laughed teasingly, delighting in his distress and then feeling sorry. 'I got out of routine with my pills but there is nothing to worry about,' kissing him soothingly, making up for the fright. 'The test was negative.'

'No wonder Chris gave me a dirty look,' he muttered, feeling weary, tired of emotional ups and downs. 'I have had enough surprises for today. Let's go home.'

On the journey Ashley outlined how she planned going about her new job. Brian listened politely while concentrating on driving. Nearing Palmer Street Ashley looked at Brian quickly when he drove straight past.

'We are not going back to Light House tonight,' answering her unspoken query. 'You have committed yourself to that place during the day. I claim you at night! If you must have night attire, you may have mine!'

Ashley didn't mind at all; their future was taking shape.

CHAPTER 9
The Changing

S pring blossomed in glorious variety and as if to make up for its tardy beginning, quickly warmed its prelude to summer.

In the doorway of the antique shop, Ernest Braithewaite breathed deeply of the soft afternoon air. He was waiting for Alfred to arrive to bank the daily takings. Up until recently it wasn't necessary to bank every day. The brothers' leisurely style of business operation had changed.

Maria and Tom at the Lunch Box and Stella Gollo were similarly placed. Fay Bennett, now in the charmingly fitted out rooms provided by Ashley, was responsible for much of the increased traffic around Light House. Her group counselling workshops brought people who after their sessions, often wanted something to eat or drink or to browse in his shop. Chris Forrest's practice had done much the same thing.

Ernest smiled to himself. Credit for the upswing in general business activity was given to Ashley for her management of the building. Without discounting her effort, he considered Brian equally responsible. He worked tirelessly setting up the consulting rooms and reception area and it was known, he steered Ashley through the intricacies of property management.

Emphatically denying any family connection to Light House at first his attitude toward the place had been uncomfortable, to say the least. However, his manner quickly softened. Ernest smiled to himself. Ashley's happiness no doubt had everything to do with that change. Exhilarating new energy permeated Light House, and Ernest could feel it stirring within himself.

Mounting the front steps of the building Helen Gilbertson came into view. Ernest remembered her from Ashley's party. Nice figure, good legs, smartly dressed, it was surprising how clear his recollection. A 'listening' type of woman he had decided at the time, noting she paid close attention to everything he told her about Light House. She also concentrated on every word Forbes Williams uttered, all the while keeping a watchful eye on Ashley and Brian.

'Hello Helen,' Ernest called stepping outside of his shop, 'how nice to see you again'! At ease with each other despite their short acquaintance they exchanged pleasantries.

'If you are looking for Ashley,' he volunteered hoping to stretch the conversation, 'she left a few minutes ago with Brian to look at another business.'

'I have an appointment with Stella,' Helen replied, 'I want her to do a boardroom lunch.' Ernest thought this another example of Brian's influence. They chatted comfortably for several minutes while he passed on news of the beauty therapy clinic that was being considered for the basement.

She is still a 'listening' type of woman he mused, gazing after her as she left to keep her appointment. Then suddenly it struck him, he wondered if she liked music.

'You are quite the little entrepreneur,' Brian remarked to Ashley that night, in reference to the use being made of Light House.

'I have been raised by storekeepers,' Ashley replied, watching him prepare their evening meal while she sipped a glass of red wine. 'Aunt Ellen and Uncle Max would expect to see the premises and their things being fully utilised!'

Warm security enfolded the pair as they gossiped in Brian's kitchen. He loved these nights at home cooking a simple meal, her bright interest and generous praise. They didn't happen as often as he would like, work keeping them in the city until late. However, they always ate dinner together. Usually something purchased from Stella and eaten at the apartment. Sometimes for a change they would go around to Ziggy's restaurant.

He showed off a little knowing it was all new to Ashley.

'Next time it's your turn,' Brian teased, finishing off his stir fry and serving it up on plates.

'I can only do steamed fish or scrambled egg,' she laughed. 'Aunt Ellen and Anna Williams never entered their respective kitchens, except to leave orders for the day. Even in the last part of her life Aunt Ellen preferred eating out, usually for lunch. Meals at home were small and extremely simple.'

'I have a surprise for you,' he announced as they sat down to dine. 'Helen is interested in purchasing your last apartment. 'She would like her mother to give up her job, rent out their home and live with Helen at Light House. She thought I would object to her proposal. I told her nothing could please me more!'

'It would please me too,' Ashley replied, disappointingly un-surprised. 'I could offer Helen's mother my receptionist job. From what I have heard she is very capable. She could adapt to the job as it grows. The hours are odd but living on the premises is convenient. I think she might jump at the opportunity.'

'Did you know Helen would take the last apartment?' Brian couldn't help noticing that things fell into place for Ashley. It was almost as if she had been planning it.

'No! But I must admit I thought it would be a good idea,' Ashley replied. They both knew of Helen's circumstances.

Owning a house was an almost impossible task for a divorced woman in the mid nineteen fifties, but Helen's mother had saved rigorously, seizing her chance when Helen was sixteen. A cheap little cottage came up for sale near the factory where she worked. Her history of thrift persuaded the bank to advance a small mortgage. Helen started working to help out her mother, finishing her education at night school. Thirty years later and surrounded by commercial enterprises, the cottage was worth many times its original value.

'I can apportion the costs of the receptionist service between the businesses. There is still room for a couple more professionals. It would be cost effective for my tenants and you and I could have dinner at home more often.'

'That sounds good to me,' Brian agreed.

'There is something else I want to ask you,' Ashley began again.

'I'm listening,' he replied affably, taking a sip of wine.

'I opened the room containing my parent's things today,' she said quietly, eyes shadowed with darkness. He well knew her fear of viewing her parent's possessions. Many times, she had woken up in the middle of the night frightened of what she might find. Soothing her as best he could, no amount of pleading to do the job for her made any difference. She refused his help, but took his comfort, all of it.

'Why now?' he asked, alarm prickling as it always did when anything appeared to threaten her. They were so happy! Why risk spoiling it by dredging up the past?

'I am ready to move on,' she replied, reading his thoughts. 'You have done that,' she added with a slow smile that made his heart race. 'The sorrow is that I know these things were packed two days before they died, and have been locked away ever since. There are some pieces I think must have belonged to my grandparents. Some things barely used. My cot and nursery furniture brought me to tears. Max and Ellen kept everything for me untouched. I cried about that too. But it was good to face up to it. I don't know why I was so afraid.' She looked at Brian with warm sincerity. 'If you agree, I would like you to have them for your house.'

Brian could only look at her.

'They need a home,' she went on, 'and I would like to keep them with me.'

'Does that mean you have settled with me for good?' It was a question he had wanted to ask for a long time, but had been too afraid.

'You won't let me live at Light House,' she teased, 'and I have nowhere else to go!'

'You can bring anything you like here,' he laughed, 'on one condition.' She looked at him questioningly.

'Marry me, Ash,' suddenly quiet and very serious. Her hesitation rocked him. His proposal had been spontaneous. He should have realised her feelings would be fragile after sorting through her parent's belongings. In an effort at light heartedness he added, 'I am a lawyer. I can't help myself. I want our union legalised and tied up in pink tape.'

'Not yet, Brian,' Ashley replied carefully, putting her fingers to his lips to stem the questions she knew would follow. 'I am enjoying my freedom. It is selfish perhaps, but I have never been free until now. I love being with you. I love what we are creating and I love our week-ends at Rocky Bay. I don't want our relationship to change, it is too precious.'

Brian remembered using a similar phrase when his father asked if they might meet his young lady.

'Not yet Dad, we haven't been together long enough. Our relationship is too fragile. I couldn't bear anything to go wrong!' It was soon after Ashley's party when Brian was visiting his parents wanting to prove there was no link between his family and Light House. They were not sure of the Christian name of their one time successful relative, it could have been Aubrey, but more likely Charles or similar. In any event they thought he was a farmer.

'We were holidaying on the south coast when you were about seven,' Robert Moore had explained as a point of interest. 'I thought we might try to find the old Harper property, but came across Rocky Bay instead. Marion and I fell in love with it. That was when we bought our allotment. We lost interest in the Harper place then and have given no thought to it since.'

It should have been a comfort to Brian but only added to his anxieties. The Deed of Title provided by Forbes showed that Aubrey Cyrus Harper registered an Encumbrance on Light House late in 1870 prohibiting its sale or transfer out of his family's estate for a period of ninety-nine years.

Ashley quickly pointed out the Encumbrance expired in 1969, around the time of their psychic experience. She also discovered from searching Public Records that Aubrey Cyrus Harper was an importer of law books, religious literature and artefacts, retiring from business about the time the

Encumbrance was raised. A few years later he died leaving a widow and two children, Charles and Emmaline. Ashley was delighted with the news. It was another flimsy scrap of circumstance that strengthened the link between Brian and Light House, and laughed when he argued to the contrary.

'What is the matter?' Ashley asked, when Brian's quiet introspective silence continued for too long.

'I have become paranoid about our relationship. My proposal was a clumsy attempt to safeguard our union. It is not right that we work all the time and then run off to Rocky Bay. I have been selfish in keeping you to myself, by not introducing you to my family and friends,' he confessed.

'So, what are you suggesting,' asked a slightly mystified Ashley who had no argument with their lifestyle. Both sets of guardians had lived similarly, although romantic week-ends were long gone when Ashley arrived on the scene.

'It's time we caught up with the real world, that's all.' he explained. 'We both have to change. It will make our love affair stronger.'

'If it makes you happy then it's all right by me,' Ashley replied agreeably.

'Right'! Brian was purposeful, 'We had better start with Mother.'

CHAPTER 10
The Sharing

'Starting with Mother,' wasn't going to be easy Brian realised, almost as soon as the words were spoken. She was very conservative in her views and would not kindly accept them openly living together.

To make matters worse Brian's father, Robert, knew his son was seriously in love with Ashley. From the verbal shorthand men exchange, he had understood how lonely and unsettled Brian had been when they first began re-designing his garden. Then, later, her name kept coming up on any pretext and the garden seemed irrelevant.

Robert began calling in every so often, just to care for the new plants, knowing Brian would be too time poor to think of them. It was he who found Ashley's things by the pool and draped them over the pool fence to dry. He was delighted with the discovery, but didn't mention it to his wife Marion.

It was easier for Brian to introduce Ashley to his long-time friend, Mike, who was now married to Jenny and they had three children.

'I thought you must have died,' Mike exclaimed cheerfully, at the sound of Brian's voice on the phone. They hadn't been to the gym or played golf for weeks.

'I have been busy; the whole firm has been busy. But I have met someone! Someone I really care about and I would like her to meet you and Jenny and your family.'

'Well come over here Saturday night, we will have a barbecue or something,' Mike offered.

'I was going to suggest a restaurant,' Brian countered, 'I thought it might be more of a treat for Jenny.'

'It would be nice for Jenny, but the littlest one has been sick, nothing serious, even so, Jen wouldn't leave him home with a sitter and taking them all out to a restaurant is a nightmare. We are much better off staying at home.'

The two men exchanged news and reminisced about bachelor days. It had been a big surprise to Brian that Mike married so soon. He always had plenty of girlfriends, most of them really glamorous, several were absolutely spectacular, but as soon as Jennifer came along, he was a changed man. Jenny was nice, but nothing special to Brian's way of thinking, however she made Mike happy. He adored his three boys; his career had soared and now he was thinking of setting up his own architectural company.

Ashley liked Jenny too. The two women enjoyed an instant rapport. Their viewpoint was similar although Jennie's was wider, probably because of their different upbringing. Jennie was from a conventional family. Ashley's altogether different.

'I liked Jennifer,' Ashley remarked to Brian driving along the highway, on the way home, 'I think they would all enjoy a week-end at Rocky Bay.'

'The children would drown in the rock pool!' Brian wasn't at all keen.

'We could take them there at low tide. They would have a marvellous time.' Ashley wasn't in the least daunted, but gave in on the argument.

'Anyway, I don't think I'm ready to share Rocky Bay just yet!' she said with a wicked grin, 'I'm not quite satisfied!'

'Why did she say that'! He nearly missed their turn-off. Arriving home, he parked the car and hurried her into the house.

'Why are you in such a rush?' she queried.

'It seems I have unfinished business,' his grin was just as wicked.

Their first social engagement being a success Brian was ready to try another one, so when his Mother phoned to ask him over for a Sunday tea, he readily agreed.

'Susan expects Gary home this week-end,' Brian's mother Marion explained, 'I thought it about time we had a family tea.'

'I would like to come, Mum, and would like to bring someone special with me,' Brian was caught unprepared. He hadn't as yet told his Mother about Ashley, or about them living together, but now it had to come out.

'Of course, you may. Who is it?'

'Her name is Ashley Preston, she was my secretary for a short time, but now is a Property Manager in the city.'

'How 'special' is she?' Marion was suddenly very curious.

'I want to marry her,' Brian decided there was no point in prevarication.

'Have you asked her?'

'Yes, but she turned me down!'

'She turned you down!' Marion's voice was sharp with amazement! 'So, what is happening now?' Marion couldn't let this conversation go.

'We are living together.' Brian was relieved his Mother had been told, whether or not she approved didn't matter.

'I am very much in love with her, Mum, and I want you to love her too. She is a special person. You will understand when you meet her.'

Marion sought out Robert, who was thankful he had not met the girl.

'I haven't seen her,' he was relieved to be able to say, 'but I am glad Brian has found someone he loves. He has been very unsettled these past few months and I have often wished a nice young woman would come along. I shall be glad to welcome her into the family.'

'But she turned him down!' Marion was dismayed.

'We don't know why! We will just have to wait to find out. Besides, it's none of our business!' Robert was a non-interventionist who had every confidence Brian would work out his own problems.

Marion wasn't so sure; already she had her doubts about Ashley.

It was family practice for all to take something for the 'tea' so Brian suggested a cake.

'What sort of cake?' Ashley wanted to know. She had never been to a 'family tea' before and felt a little nervous. Brian wasn't much help.

'Any sort will do. You are new and anything you bring will be new too, so please yourself!'

Ashley consulted Stella Gollo, who suggested an apple and cream torte and offered to make it, so that was settled.

Then she worried about what she should wear and spent a long time choosing a suitable dress, finally selecting a very conservative, navy and white floral creation with a full skirt, demure neckline, and short sleeves. Stylish wedge heeled sandals completed the picture.

Brian thought she looked absolutely gorgeous. His eye took in not the attire so much, but the woman herself. She was a pleasure to behold, soft skin, colourful hair, slim body, lovely bosom, great legs, healthy tan.

'I wish we were going to Rocky Bay instead,' Ashley said, catching his warm appraisal.

'Me too,' looking at his watch, but it was time to get going.

Robert and Marion met them at the front door where Brian introduced his parents.

They all moved along to the living room, where Susan and Gary and their two small boys joined in the introductions.

Ashley handed over the cake. Marion took

a peek and was very impressed.

'Did you make this cake?' she asked.

'No, cooking isn't my forte,' Ashley replied honestly, 'I had someone make it for me.'

'Brian says you and he are living together, so who does the cooking in your house?' Marion asked.

'Brian mostly, I suppose,' Ashley replied candidly, 'sometimes we buy a meal or go out to a restaurant.'

Marion didn't make further comment, but Ashley was quick to detect underlying disapproval.

Susan was much friendlier. She called up her little boys, Thomas and Geoffrey, explained that Brian called them 'Tom and Jerry' and often took them out to McDonalds for tea when their Daddy was away.

'Where does your husband work?' Ashley was interested.

'At the Pilbara! He's a mining engineer. He works three weeks and then has a week off.'

'It must be lonely for you at times,' Ashley remarked sympathetically.

'It is,' Susan agreed, 'I wanted to go up there with him, but he said living there is too rugged, too hot and uncomfortable. He wouldn't want to put me and the two boys under that stress.'

'You are under stress either way,' Ashley remarked,' it can't be easy looking after two little boys, a house and all that goes with it, by yourself.' Ashley then pulled herself up. She should keep her opinion to herself and say no more. It was none of her business.

The family tea proceeded slowly to its conclusion, everyone started leaving by about nine o'clock and Ashley and Brian were glad to get back home.

Preparing to retire, Ashley was seated at the dressing-table brushing her hair, Brian already in bed watching her.

'I like your family, Brian they seem to be close and get along well together.' Ashley remarked.

'Mum has Susan under her thumb. One day Sue will tire of doing things Mum's way and then there will be an upheaval and feelings will be hurt. Sue asked for my opinion about shifting to the Pilbara with Gary. I told her that she should keep her family together. She chose to ignore my advice.' Brian declared flatly.

'But Sue said Gary thought the Pilbara too stressful for their little family?' Ashley was puzzled.

'They both want the money. It will set them up for the future. Sure, it's hot and rugged, but the homes provided for staff are comfortable and there are plenty of social set-ups to make life easier. They could all be in the adventure together. There would be no more loneliness for either of them and the boys would have their Mum and Dad. I think Mother had a hand in Sue's refusal to go with Gary. I wouldn't want her interfering with my life!'

Brian's forthright response surprised Ashley. Marion must be a force to be considered, she made a mental note to treat her with caution. She also decided it best to change the subject.

'Brian, tomorrow I intend to start going through my parent's things. Is it still alright to bring them here?'

'I told you the conditions,' he replied, not taking his eyes from her.

'I know and I agree in principle. I just want to enjoy our 'affair' a little longer.'

'Well, I'm ready. How long are you going to keep me waiting?' he asked, raising the covers.

Laughing, she slipped into his warm bed.

CHAPTER 11
The Finding

Braithewaites were called on to go through the old consignment and were excited by the contents. The most valuable piece was a Thomas Chippendale Mahogany bookcase in Gothic style. The other items were two dressers, lounge, dining, kitchen and bedroom furniture, a handsome bureau, ladies writing desk and sundry chairs and tables. All needed refurbishment to some extent. Then there was an assortment of household linen, crockery, cutlery, pots and pans. Ashley would have to choose what she wanted to keep and probably auction the remainder.

'Brian?' Ashley queried, as she was setting the end of their dining table in Light House for one of Stella's take-away meals. He was at the other end busy sorting through papers drawn from his briefcase.

They had put Marion out of their minds, her implied disapproval meant nothing to them they were too richly involved with their daily work, the ongoing development of Light House and several side issues that were beginning to emerge.

'Yes,' he answered absently.

'The interior of your house needs to be re-painted,' she decided not to bore him with details.

'It was painted just a few years ago, when Mike designed the alterations!' he sounded mystified.

'The part we live in is fine,' she replied, 'but your formal lounge, dining room, entry and spare bedrooms haven't been touched since the house was built, I would guess.' Ashley knew she was right.

'I know I have agreed to you bringing your furniture here, but surely it is un-necessary to re-paint the house simply for storage?

'I am not simply storing it. I am preparing it for use!' Ashley kept her manner matter-of-fact. She didn't want to annoy Brian but he was immersed in the present, it was time to look to the future.

'Why?' he asked.

'Because you are a senior partner and soon Charles will be looking to you to entertain clients. Jack Henderson comes to mind; he and his wife are family oriented and would appreciate being invited to your house.'

'You are forgetting one thing,' Brian smugly replied. 'Henderson and his wife are as old-fashioned as Mother. You are only my girl-friend. They wouldn't be impressed by being entertained by a 'de-facto.'

His remark shocked Ashley, and adding to the hurt, she realised he was right.

He saw her deflation and immediately regretted his comment. He apologised, but she waved aside his remarks.

'You are right! They wouldn't be impressed and nor would my parents if they were alive, or my Aunt and Uncle. I have been very selfish.'

She sat quietly reconsidering her situation.

'Ashley, you can paint the rooms any colour you like, I just want you to be happy,' Brian didn't know what else to say.

From that point in time the house seemed to be full of tradesmen. In the middle of the painting period, when Brian's house reeked of paint and Ashley still adamant, they should never sleep together at Light House, Charles asked if Brian would stand in for him at a Law Convention to be held in Sydney this next week-end.

Brian jumped at the chance, suggesting that he took Ashley with him, at his own expense. Charles was agreeable, he considered Ashley well connected and liked the idea of promoting his firm to a well-known QC in Sydney.

Ashley was delighted to be visiting Sydney for a few days, but as there was no time for shopping, she would have to be satisfied with her existing wardrobe. It was while she was going through the clothing still kept at Light House, she came across the last item Max had made for her, a beautifully tailored suit in white Thai silk. She put it aside for packing and then rediscovered the gown bought on impulse from Medici's.

'Look Brian, at what I have found!' she was holding it against herself as she had done before, in his office.

He remembered it, only too well! How jealous he had been at the time; it had spoiled his entire week-end.

'Where did you go when you wore that dress,' that same sick feeling was coming back, but he had to know.

'I've never worn it anywhere. It's still got the ticket on it! I just loved it and couldn't resist buying it.'

'Make sure you bring it with you. We will have a really special night out, dinner, dancing and a bit of glamour.'

Brian booked a suite and for a couple of extra days too. He admitted it was an extravagance, but he felt like indulging in a bit of luxury.

Their suite boasted a spa-bath. It was an unexpected treat for Ashley who spurned the swimming pool and revelled in the spa instead. She looked so utterly delicious with her hair piled high on her head and up to her shoulders in bubbles, Brian couldn't resist joining in. The Convention was off to a very good start and it had nothing at all to do with the Law.

Later, handsome in dinner jacket and bow tie, and pouring two glasses of French champagne, Brian glanced up as Ashley entered the room. Still softly aglow from their love-making and wearing the white dress that delicately enhanced every curve of her body, she simply took his breath away.

Ashley had done that to him before, many times, but tonight was different. Tonight, he wanted this evening to be special. He wanted to know if their 'affair' as she described it, was as exciting for her as it was for him. She looked like a woman very much loved, but was she a woman 'in love'. He desperately needed to know.

'You are a dream come true,' he finally managed to say. Getting his voice back he added, 'I often think about our original meeting and am no closer to an explanation of it, but you really are a dream come true!'

'So are you,' she answered as they touched glasses. 'Let's drink to 'dreams coming true!'

'I have bought you something,' he said as they sipped their champagne, 'I didn't know when to give it to you, or if I should, but I want you to have it,' handing her a small box. Opening it slowly, she gasped when she saw it contained a beautiful diamond ring.

'Brian,' she whispered, 'I think it's the loveliest ring I have ever seen,' she looked at him questioningly.

'I acknowledge I agreed we would discuss marriage later, but I am completely in love with you and I need to know if you really love me. If I can see you wearing my ring, then I will be happier about waiting.'

Ashley looked at him intensely, there was no doubt he meant every word he said. She felt a surge of excitement, of surety.

'Of course, I will! I don't really know why I have hesitated. I am in love with you too and I will be proud to be your wife!'

She handed him back the box so that he could put the ring on her finger. He did so with much ceremony.

Ashley phoned Forbes and Anna to tell them of her engagement and they were both pleased to hear the news.

'So, when do you propose to marry?' Forbes wanted to know.

'We haven't thought about that yet. I just wanted to let you know that we are engaged.'

'Let me have a word with Brian,' said Forbes. Ashley handed over the phone.

'Brian, I've just been told the good news. I must say I am pleased to hear it. I'm going to suggest you marry here, while in Sydney. I can make all the arrangements and have a celebrant in our house. I think it would be good for Ashley to launch this next part of her life from somewhere where she has always been safe and secure. Think about what I have said and let me know. Congratulations to you both!'

Brian put down the phone thoughtfully.

'Forbes has recommended we marry while

we are here, in Sydney,' he stated the suggestion plainly, giving no indication of his opinion.

'Why?' Ashley was puzzled.

Brian repeated the details of the conversation he had with Forbes. Ashley listened quietly, without taking her eyes from Brian's face.

'What is your opinion?' she asked.

'I think it the perfect suggestion for us. You must admit our love affair has been anything but ordinary. Your life has been anything but ordinary. I like the idea of launching your new life from a place of safety and security. It seems to auger stability for the future.' He waited for a few moments allowing time for her to digest the proposal. Then he joined her on the couch, took her hands in his and asked again, 'Will you marry me, Ashley?'

'Yes,' she replied softly, 'but not for quite the same reasons as you have outlined,' she touched his face softly to take away the slight frown that appeared on his brow.

'When I was packing, I came across a suit Max made for me years ago, I brought it with me on impulse. It will be perfect for a wedding. I feel I have their blessing.'

Brian phoned Forbes; it was the most satisfying phone call of his entire life.

'Forbes says he needs twenty-four hours and will contact us tomorrow with details!'

'As this is the first and last night of our engagement,' he declared to Ashley, offering his arm, 'let's make it a beautiful celebration.'

The ceremony at Forbes house was a delight. Held on the patio off the lounge room where there were sweeping views of the Harbour, Forbes had placed a side-table covered by a fine leather mat to be used as a desk, on which was placed a Bible and writing set. Soft music drifted out from the lounge room. The Celebrant and her assistant arrived at the appointed time with a Registration book and other papers to be signed.

The Celebrant and her assistant stood behind the table, Brian and Ashley stood before it and Forbes and Anna sat on chairs to the side.

The age-old words of the Marriage Ceremony were spoken, the age-old questions were asked of the bride and groom and the age-old vows were taken. Forbes and Anna were called on as witnesses and Brian and Ashley were pronounced 'man and wife'.

Afterwards they all retired to the lounge room where the newly married couple were 'toasted' with champagne by all present. The Celebrant and her assistant stayed for a short time and then moved on to another appointment.

The bridal party retired to 'The Anchorage', a very fine restaurant also overlooking the Harbour and renowned for its excellent cuisine. It was an entirely beautiful occasion, followed by a completely ecstatic two-day honeymoon for the bride and groom that knew no set pattern, or programme.

'I'll have to reimburse Charles for the whole cost of the Convention,' Brian commented to Ashley. They were well on their way home, due to 'touch-down' in about an hour. 'I didn't take any interest in it at all. I was obsessed with you the whole time. When Forbes suggested we marry I couldn't believe you would agree. I couldn't believe it when you did. I kept thinking we were having another 'psychic experience'.

'Charles will be pleased you have made a friend in Forbes; he will see that as a benefit to the firm.' Ashley was quite sure Charles would be satisfied to know Brian and Forbes were on very good terms.

Back home the painting was finished, and there was a message from Braithwaite's saying the furniture was ready for delivery.

There was also a box addressed to Ashley labelled 'Assorted Stationery and Letter to be replaced in Ladies Writing Desk'. Curiosity aroused, she lifted the lid on the unsealed box and there on the top in a plain white envelope, now yellowed with age, was a letter addressed to 'My Darling Ashley'.

Something struck at her heart. Her body went still, her blood ebbed. She sat down on a chair, deathly pale.

Nearby, Brian had seen her open the box and was frightened by her re-action.

'What's the matter?' he asked urgently, coming to her side, fiercely protective. Anything that affected Ashley panicked him.

Still unable to speak, she showed him the un-opened letter. He examined it carefully.

'Braithewaites' must have found it when they were re-polishing the furniture. We know it has been in storage for twenty-five years so the letter has been locked away at least that long. The hand writing looks feminine to me, so my guess it is something for you from your mother.'

He noticed her colour coming back so, deliberately kept his voice low and soothing.

'Go over to the settee and make yourself comfortable while I make us some coffee, then we will read the letter together.'

CHAPTER 12
The Letter

They settled into a corner of the settee. Aware of her nervous tension, he drew her in close, one arm around her, letter in the other hand

'Here goes,' he said, ready at last.

'My Darling Ashley,

It is Sunday 31st May, 1953, I have just given you your last feed for the night and you are sleeping in your bassinet like an angel. Your daddy is asleep too, in our bed. We have been so busy these last few weeks preparing for our trip to Glenbourne.

I don't know why I feel compelled to tell you this now, you certainly aren't old enough to understand what I am saying, but one day you might be pleased to hear a little of your history.

Your daddy comes from a small but comfortable family who have been in the tailoring trade for decades. Sadly, just before you were born your grand-parents died, leaving just Uncle Max and Aunt Ellen as our only living relatives. That is the reason why we are moving to Glenbourne, so all the Prestons can be together.

My history is quite different from that of your father's. My mother was a foundling. She was left on the steps of the Adelaide Children's Home in March, 1870, in a packing crate. Dressed in good quality clothing and finely knitted garments, it was thought she may have come from a good family. These items were kept by the home as they were the only clues to the baby's identity.

They named her Angela, because she looked like an angel and gave her the surname of March, because of the time of the year she arrived at the home.

From a very early age Angela was observed to have a unique manner with the other children. As she grew older this practise expanded. She was good at getting them to do their work or their study. Instead of putting her out to work at twelve years of age, as was the rule in those times, she was retained by the home as a Teacher's Helper.

She was fourteen years old when the Reverend Samuels and his wife took over the management of the home. They were newly arrived from England and had no family of their own overseas, or here in Australia, and so they took an interest in Angela.

When Angela was sixteen, they tried to help her to find a clue to her origins and brought the crate out of the cellar into the bright light of day. There was a mark stamped on the end of the crate that had been almost, but not entirely sanded off. The local green grocer suggested it may have come from the Harper Estate, which had been a large land holding down south in the Willunga area.

The Samuels found an address for the Estate and gave Angela permission to travel there for an interview with the current resident. It led to an appointment with a woman, who upon seeing Angela became so scathingly bitter and resentful, Angela left in tears.

She returned to the orphanage, still unclear about her origins and very upset. She was kindly received and remained there for the rest of her life.

In 1915, when Angela was forty-five years old, she married Reverend Samuels who had been widowed the previous year and was a man of about sixty years of age. Angela became pregnant in 1918 and died giving birth to me. She would have been forty-eight. Reverend Samuels christened me 'Angelina', in honour of my Mother.

I do not remember my own early childhood. I can only say I must have been happy. Reverend Samuels as my father was a kindly man. He too came from a small family in England. To my knowledge there was never any communication from overseas.

As I grew up, he relied on me more and more. It was good training, because when he died in 1942, I was twenty-four and confident enough to leave the orphanage, find a flat in Adelaide and a job as a clerk with a wholesale fabric company. It was there I met your father.

Our story is uncomplicated. We met, fell in love, married and now we have you, whom we named 'Ashley' simply because we liked it, and are excited by our new life about to unfold in Glenbourne.

My eternal love,
Your mother,
 Angelina.

Brian and Ashley stirred on the couch. He was cramped and stiff, Ashley in tears.

'That name has come up again,' Brian remarked, referring to 'Harper'. 'But it hasn't proved anything. All it has proved is that your grandmother was a foundling.'

'It has provided another avenue to explore though,' Ashley insisted. 'Your mother said she thought your successful relatives were farmers, perhaps they were orchardists?'

'I don't know,' said Brian, 'I'm tired of the past! My only care is our future. Have you decided what are you going to do with all this furniture Braithwaite's are waiting to deliver?'

CHAPTER 13
The Gifting

The next few weeks were chaotic. Ashley spent most of her time at Brian's house with decorators, carpet layers, curtain fitters, light fitters and Braithwaite's men bringing in as many pieces of furniture as could be placed.

Ashley's role at Light House had altered somewhat since Helen and her mother Moira moved in.

Moira gladly took on the role of Receptionist, with a desk being provided in the main entry of the building. All she had to do was direct patients or clients to the appropriate rooms, take delivery of any parcels, pass them on and answer telephone enquiries.

She also took it upon herself to take care of the indoor plants, it was something she liked doing. The job paid her a nice wage and as she was meeting a variety of people, it was necessary to look neat and tidy, so she took a renewed interest in her appearance.

Helen was happier too, she could walk to work, her Mother was re-energised and their finances considerably improved with the rent from their old house and her mother's wage.

Ashley made an office for herself in her upstairs lobby, she intended working there once she was finished with the re-decoration of Brian's house. Light House was now completely operational and there was a different set of clerical duties to perform. Brian guided her on these matters knowing that once they were instigated, she could be left to their management.

Mainly he kept well away from Light House, only picking her up at night whenever necessary, to take her home. He admired what she was doing.

Every week at his house there was progress

and she took a delight in showing each step as it was finalised.

The ladies writing desk she put into their bedroom. Nothing else had been changed, but it looked lovely and added a touch of elegance to the room.

The three spare bedrooms had been re-organised. They were now a single and a double bedroom, the other had been made into a small sitting room. It was a cosy and comfortable arrangement. That part of the house also contained a bathroom and the laundry.

His own study had been re-organised, a matter that created much angst until he realised it worked better.

Connected by double doors that had previously been kept closed, the dining room and lounge room with the doors opened, appeared to merge. Mahogany furniture gleamed richly in both rooms. A handsome table, a set of chairs and both dressers were placed in the dining room. The Chippendale bookcase took pride of place in the lounge. There were two settees, set conversation style in front of the fireplace and several comfortable arm chairs placed about the room. Most were upholstered in soft beige suede.

The rooms looked rich, conservative and comfortable. Ashley intended bringing in colour with art works and had asked Anna Williams' advice.

'I think we are almost ready to invite a few guests for dinner,' she cheekily informed Brian when she was showing him the finished rooms.

'I'm very impressed,' he remarked, looking around in appreciation, 'I didn't think it would come up like this! You must have spent a small fortune.'

'Just a small one,' she agreed, 'but worth every cent. It's our home and my contribution towards it.'

'Now we have this most impressive dining room,' he teased, 'have you given any thought to what we might have for dinner tonight?'

'Yes, Mr. Smartie Pants, I have thought about it. We are having scrambled eggs!'

It marked the beginning of a brand-new lifestyle for them both. They revelled in being married, life was rich and full and fun.

Their first formal dinner party was held to announce their marriage to his fellow senior partners and their wives, to introduce Ashley to that group of people.

The next one was to entertain Jack Henderson and his wife. Charles, of course needed to be present, as well two other senior partners, who did occasional work for Henderson, all with their wives, as well as Consultant, Angus McIntyre, a single gentleman whom Helen had agreed to partner for the evening.

On both of these occasions Stella was employed to do the catering, on both occasions impressing the guests with the quality and style of food. For the service of it she hired her nephew to assist with both the food and wine. Ashley was comfortable with this type of entertaining, it was what she was accustomed to in Forbes' home.

Summer arrived and they began to make use of their pool and garden. A family barbecue was organised and Brian invited Mike and his family to come too. Five little boys running around were a handful, but they all had a glorious time. They were better in the pool where Ashley kept a sharp look-out for trouble. Jennifer and Susan were instantly friendly. They had a lot in common and a lot of information to share about raising boys. When they joined the children in the pool, Ashley donned her beach-coat and offered to show Marion around the house again. It was something Marion liked to do and about the only thing Ashley did that Marion admired.

It had come as a shock to her that Ashley and Brian had married so suddenly.

It was also a great disappointment. She would have loved a big wedding. Brian knew important people; it could have been a grand occasion and she would have had a prominent role to play. For them to get engaged one day and married the next and not tell his parents until they arrived home was an insult. She didn't like Ashley very much. She didn't really know why; it was an instinctive thing.

'Yes, I would like to see how it's coming along,' she said pleasantly enough when asked, 'I haven't seen it since just after you came home from Sydney and there was furniture stowed everywhere.'

'I hope you approve,' Ashley was being as nice as possible, she was aware of Marion's dislike and doing her best to dissolve it. 'If we go in through the front door the effect is better.'

They stepped into the entry and there was Brian's study on the right. Marion had already seen that and liked it very much. It suited her son, all polished wood and black leather. Bookcases lining the walls full of books, curios and a few photos. One of their family, taken years ago, when they were all down at Rocky Bay.

Crossing the entry Ashley opened the sliding glass doors to the lounge. She stood aside to allow the older woman to pass.

'I didn't think it was such a large room,' Marion was astonished.

'It looks bigger because the dining room doors are open,' Marion then noticed that they were. Brian had always kept them shut because that part of the house was unused.

'This is the dining room,' Ashley explained

unnecessarily, and Marion walked in admiring the beautiful furniture.

'You will be able to have some very elegant dinner parties here,' Marion observed, obviously very impressed.

'Yes, we have already had two,' Ashley volunteered, 'One for Brian's partners and one for his most important client!'

Marion was silent. 'His workmates are entertained in style while his family are consigned to the garden!'

It was as if Ashley could read Marion's mind and she was ready for the next barb.

'Who did the cooking?' Marion enquired.

'Neither of us,' Ashley pointed out. 'We hired a caterer, because they were business dinners, and as such are taxation deductions.' Ashley hoped that would silence Marion.

Overall, the day was a success. Ashley did not mention Marion's comment to Brian, deeming it too trivial.

The style of the day became a template for many more such occasions over the summer. He invited his colleagues and their families to enjoy the garden and pool while all pitched in to cook on the barbecue, then laze about around a long table set up under the shade of the trees.

Sometimes Mike and his family joined in. Mike knew a few of Brian's colleagues from University days, when they were all bachelors, so there were some good tales to tell around the barbecue. It was all very casual and that was the greatest appeal. Away from the strict discipline of the Law, informality was a rare prize.

Stella Gollo was frequently called upon to be present at these casual functions. Sometimes they had a large piece of meat to be barbecued and she was the best one to prepare it and cook it in her portable oven.

At other times she would provide a simple sweet like an apple pie or a rhubarb tart, but they were ones big enough to serve all the guests. Her expertise with cooking attracted a keen admirer.

Angus MacIntyre, the Consultant often engaged by Syms Simcock on special cases and who was present at Brian and Ashley's second formal dinner, was absolutely fascinated by Stella. He followed her around all afternoon at these casual events and helped her clean up afterwards, a detail not unobserved by the other guests. It even raised quiet speculation as to whether or not 'he would make a move'.

Angus was about fifty, unmarried, in fact had never been married, and was an expert in Commercial Law. He lived alone in a comfortable house in one of the outer suburbs along the coast.

He loved food, and asked Stella if she would cook a special meal for him. She agreed and they discussed pre-dinner drinks and nibbles. He liked scotch best and would take her suggestion for a lady, so Stella suggested champagne as that usually suited most women.

He wasn't too keen on nibbles either, so left it to Stella to provide a plate of savoury biscuits. The main course he was settled on, he wanted Beef Wellington, and he wanted a large sized piece of beef, with all the usual accompaniments, roast potato, carrots, parsnips, beans and horseradish sauce. For sweets he wanted something creamy and left that too, to Stella.

'How many guests' Stella asked?

'Two', he replied.

Stella was rather perplexed. He wanted dinner served at seven. For such a large piece of beef she would have to get to his place at four in the afternoon to give it time to cook. The other things would only take a short time to prepare, which meant she would be sitting around for hours with nothing to do. She decided to give him an exorbitant quote, reasoning that he as a lawyer would know he was being cheated and as a Scotsman he would be outraged, thus her quote would be rejected and she could forget about the whole thing.

However, he happily accepted the price and paid in advance. Stella was amazed.

She was further amazed when on arriving in her catering van at the appointed time, dressed, ready for work, she discovered that 'she' was the guest.

He refused to accept a refund of the money and instead offered to help her do the cooking. He prepared the vegetables while she quickly made the pastry to wrap around the beef. It didn't take long to set it going and then there was nothing much else left to do, so he suggested a scotch and offered Stella champagne.

They settled down in the kitchen and started talking. They talked endlessly. They talked about food, about opinions, about their history, about their current life and their past life. They talked about their empty future. They opened another bottle of champagne and suddenly it all seemed hilariously funny.

Dinner was served and it was delicious. He helped her to clean-up the kitchen and to do the dishes. Then it was late and time to go home, but he worried about Stella driving at night as 'there are so many dangers on the road'.

He offered her the spare bed.

'I would rather sleep in yours,' she replied. So that settled the matter. They both agreed; it was the best evening they each had enjoyed for a long, long time.

Light House was beginning to have an

effect on all connected with the place. All of the businesses were doing well and 'nothing breeds success like success.' Prosperity was beginning to shine in many different ways. The general mood about the place was upbeat, people were smiling and helpful.

Helen Gilbertson's mother's interest in gardening had prompted her to offer to look after the indoor plants, but some of the pots were large and heavy. Alfred Braithewaite, the elder of the two brothers saw her struggling one day to shift one, and immediately came to her aid. It started off a friendship that would last for the rest of their lives. Alfred was a gardener too. He loved nothing more than pottering around in his shed and tending to his plants.

'It's the only thing I miss from my home,' Moira confessed. 'My apartment is much more comfortable than my house ever was, but I do miss a garden.'

The following Sunday, Moira and Helen were invited to view Alfred's garden and to take afternoon tea with the brothers. The weather was fine, so they sat outside on the veranda where Ernest had set up a pretty tea table. It was a new experience for both women as they had not taken a proper old-fashioned tea before. They found the experience charming.

Light House was expanding its effect on its inhabitants and no one could say it wasn't for the better.

CHAPTER 14
The Passing

The next few years passed by swiftly.

Life was rich, old friendships were maintained and new ones made. Business continued to prosper at Light House and the throughout the city in general. Brian, next in line to be Managing Partner of Syms Simcock, after Charles relinquished the reins, was content with his own clients and in no hurry for change.

Ashley, still the delight of his life, was managing Light House very well. All of her original apartment dwellers were still in place. The only movement noticed among her occupants was personal to them and did not show any signs of an impending change to her list of tenants.

Moira Gilbertson, depending upon the weather, spent an occasional week-end of gardening with Alfred Braithewaite at his house. Ernest Braithewaite always managed to have theatre or concert tickets available at these times and shared them with Helen Gilbertson. It was a pleasant diversion for them all. They had each grown used to a lonely life, and now they were becoming accustomed to company, in measured doses.

Stella was still cooking up a storm with Angus McIntyre, but showed no sign of giving up her independence. However, you could see that Angas wanted more of her company and was patiently waiting for the right circumstances to evolve.

Jack Henderson's empire was out-growing every other conglomerate in the State, keeping Brian extremely busy, which in turn benefited Syms Simcock.

The only cloud on the horizon was Marion who still harboured feelings of antipathy toward Ashley.

Susan had long since decided to keep her

family together and had joined her husband, Gary, in the Pilbara. This decision was made only a few months after meeting Ashley. It was seeing her brother's new found happiness that changed Susan's mind.

'It is rugged,' she wrote, 'but not as bad as I thought it would be.'

Robert was pleased with the arrangement, as he had offered to, and was kept busy collecting the rent from his daughter's house and to seeing to any maintenance matters that arose.

Marion was bitterly disappointed. Not only had she lost her daughter and grandchildren, she had no other interest to fill the gap in her life. It didn't occur to her to look for something else, she just blamed Ashley.

'Who have you got among your family and friends that we could invite for a small dinner party?' Ashley enquired of Brian one evening when they were having a rare night relaxing in front of the television.

'Why?' he wanted to know.

'I'm worried about your Mother. She is still resentful of me and blames me for Susan and the children going away. I thought a dinner party might cheer her up,' Ashley started to explain.

'Sue has been gone for years! Anyway, I told Sue to keep her family together!' Brian asserted, 'Mum knows that'!

'Yes, but I said something too! It was when I first met Sue at your parent's home.' Ashley was trying to understand Marion's resentment and wanting to do something about it.

'That was seven years ago!' Brian was surprised. 'Do you realise we have been together seven years!'

'It's a bit more actually. We had been living together for a few months before I was introduced to your family,' Ashley was remembering too. 'I couldn't cook then and Stella made me an elaborate cake to take to the family tea. It didn't impress Marion. It would have done, had I made it.' She sounded regretful.

'Don't let Mother get you down,' Brian sympathised warmly, 'I know what would cheer her up more than a dinner party.'

'I do too', Ashley returned, 'a grandchild. Have you given any thought to having a family?'

'Quite honestly, no,' he admitted. 'I like children, I really do and I miss Susan's boys. I like Mike's boys too, but children can take an enormous slice out of your life. I know they give it back a thousandfold, or so I've been told, but both of the sets of parents we are talking about seem to have missed out on the closeness we share. So, I am not really fussed about having a family, unless of course, you are ready.'

'I don't know whether I want to or not,' Ashley was being honest too. 'I have mixed feelings, sometimes I think I would love to have a little baby, other times I am not sure, even worse, I am fearful.'

'That settles it then,' Brian declared, 'I don't want you having to face up to anything that frightens you. I couldn't bear it if anything went wrong, or worse, if something happened to you.'

'Do you realise we haven't been to Rocky Bay for a week-end for more than a year?' Ashley remarked, sitting alongside him on the settee and making herself comfortable. She knew exactly how to do it, wriggling in close, pulling his arms around her like a shawl.

'Minx!' he whispered, cuddling her close, 'you treat me like an old cardigan'.

'I've got a hectic two weeks coming up. Jack Henderson is interested in acquiring a steel manufacturing business in Mt. Gambier. He wants me to go down there with him to check it over. It means I will be away from you for that time.

'Why Mt. Gambier?' Ashley queried.

'Because it is halfway between Adelaide and Melbourne, Jack has a small plant here in Adelaide and is thinking of merging the two. It means he will be closer to a much bigger market.'

Brian didn't take long to organise himself once his mind was made up.

'I will make sure I have this week-end free, pick you up from Light House and we can drive down to Rocky Bay Friday afternoon. What do you say about that?'

'I would absolutely love it,' Ashley whispered back, 'I'll get Stella to pack us a hamper like the one she made up for us the first time we went to Rocky Bay.'

Brian still had a black sports car, a later model, bigger, sleeker and faster with all the latest devices. The old one he gave to Ashley, who more often than not kept it parked at Light House.

'You should sell it,' she had remarked at the time.

'I can't bear to part with it,' he had said, giving her the keys, 'it means too much to me.'

Stella beamed when she handed over the hamper, reminding them again of that first trip to Rocky Bay. Brian put down the hood and they were off, patiently through the City traffic, carefully out of the suburbs, more quickly along the outskirts of the metropolitan area, then skimming along the dips and rises of the open road, wind in their faces, freedom to relish and share.

Some of the little towns along the way were a bit bigger, but the nearer to Rocky Bay, the more unchanged the scenery. They turned off the highway onto the dirt road still rough from last winter's wet weather. They stopped at the crest of the hill. The two houses were still there, unchanged, as well as the tamarisk trees. The rocks and the bay were unaltered and so too their little house.

Within minutes they had unpacked the car, turned on the power and were out on the sand excited as children. They splashed through the shallows, climbed over the rocks until they were on the ledge just above the pool. Ashley immediately started stripping off her clothes.

'I think we are in for some rough weather,' said Brian, looking at black clouds looming on the horizon. The ocean sounded extremely loud and different, the pool was cloudy and restless.

'I don't care,' she laughed, diving in.

Almost as she dived a giant green-grey wave reared up over the rocks and slammed down on the pool. Brian was knocked off his feet and drenched to the skin, but he thought nothing of that, his only thought was for Ashley. He couldn't see her!

Screaming her name, he wiped the water from his face and tried to focus. The sea was roaring and the pool white with foam. He couldn't see her. He was still screaming her name as the wave rushed out. Another came in almost as big, swamping the ledge and in receding took some of the foam.

He thought he saw her legs and jumped in. Something tried to grasp at his leg. He reached down blindly and felt her hair, grabbing it he pulled her up by the hair until he could get a stronger grip around her body. Treading water, he pushed her to the ledge. Where his strength came from, he didn't know, but he had enough to get her arms onto the ledge, then she started to cough and splutter, heaving to draw breath. He clambered up on the rock and pulled her out of the water.

Taking off his sweater he tried to help her into it, but it was wet and unworkable and she still helpless, gasping for breath. Looking toward the horizon he saw the black storm clouds almost upon them and knew to get out of this place as fast possible. Pulling Ashley up to face him he managed to hoist her over his shoulder in a fireman's grip, climbed back over the rocks and trudged urgently back to the house. Hearing her choking and spluttering he hoped some of the water she would have swallowed was draining out.

He lowered Ashley down on the settee and then hunted in the closet for a towel and a soft warm rug. Wrapping the towel around her head and tucking the rug about her, he then searched in another cupboard for a bottle of scotch. She was breathing normally now and looked a little better.

Quickly he made a pot of tea, adding a very generous splash of scotch. He poured out a mug full, added milk and sugar and brought it to her on the couch.

'Put some dry clothes on, Brian,' she croaked, 'you will catch a cold!'

She had just had a near death experience and worried about him catching cold! It almost broke his composure.

'Right'! He said, noticing he was still soaked to the skin and hurried into the laundry. He stripped off his clothing, raced upstairs, found undies and tracksuit and put them on. He found similar things for Ashley and took them back downstairs. She had just finished her mug of tea.

'Let me help you with these!' She was still unsteady and held onto Brian while he helped her into the garments. He decided it would be better to put her to bed and carried her up to their bedroom, tucked her in, adding a big soft eiderdown for extra warmth.

'Would you like something to eat?' he asked, unsure of what to do next.

'No, thanks, I would just like to be quiet for a while. Perhaps later,' she sounded exhausted.

'Right'! He said, 'That goes for me too,' quickly undressing, climbing into their bed and holding her close, like a father would to comfort his child. It was enough, for the time, to be dry, warm, and safe.

The storm moved in, engulfing Rocky Bay. The wind shrieked, rain lashed down and the sea was in a frenzy. The ancient granite rocks, with dour determination, faced whatever the storm threw at them in contemptuous silence. So too the three little grey weathered wooden houses.

It raged nearly all night. Not until morning had it worn itself out, leaving the sea rattled, but trying to resume its usual conversation with the shore. It was the comparative quiet that awakened Ashley. She could feel Brian's heartbeat, fast and strong and knew he was still upset. He was immediately aware of her wakefulness.

'Are you alright, Ashley?' it was his first concern.

'Yes, I feel quite well, thanks to you,' she turned over within his arms, kissing him softly about the neck.

'I know Rocky Bay is reputed to be dangerous, but in all the years we have been coming here I have never seen the ocean like it was yesterday. We must have been hit by two freak waves. You were swallowed up. I thought you were gone! It was a nightmare! If you had been swept away or drowned, I couldn't go on, I wouldn't want to! 'I never want to experience anything like that again.'

She could feel his distress, his fright of what might have been. He had saved her life with no regard for his own and looked after her when she couldn't look after herself.

He needed to be comforted. She kissed him again, urgently, he knew her too well to mistake the signals. He thought he remembered asking her 'if she was sure', but it soon became obvious she was and that they needed each other.

The rest of the week-end passed by uneventfully, they didn't go to the pool again, not even for a look to see if there had been any change. Content with basking in the sunshine on warm sand or a quick dip in the ocean from the broader beach their relationship touched a new depth.

There was one other occurrence. A persistent banging disturbed them on the night after the storm. Brian checked around and all appeared to be in order. Looking further afield he saw the gate to the two little houses sagging and loose.

Collecting a few tools, he went over to the houses to fix the gate. Being nosey and understandably curious, Ashley went with him to have a look around.

'These really are two separate houses,' Brian exclaimed, 'two rooms each, living room and sleeping room I guess.'

'I wonder you never checked them out when you were younger!' Ashley exclaimed.

'Mum was a stickler for privacy and so too was Dad. Anyway, they thought it none of their business and we were too busy building our own to worry about the empty houses next door.'

Ashley was not so high-minded. Something about the houses, now that she was standing next to them, on their ground, excited her curiosity. She began exploring the little garden, just a couple of small beds at the base of the cliff face that may have been used for vegetables or suchlike. There was another smaller bed, where the cliff turned towards the sea. It was overgrown with wild couch grass. You could see where once there had been a border, fragments of it remained. At the top you could see a stone, now covered with tough wild couch grass. She started pulling out the grass.

'Ashley, what are you doing?' Brian had seen her intense activity and had come to investigate.

'I want to uncover this rock,' she said not looking up, but pulling at the grass feverishly.

'Don't ask me 'why'! I don't know, but I must!' she continued working.

He helped her by loosening some of the grass around the rock with his screwdriver. A few minutes later they had loosened enough of the grass to uncover the stone, roughly the size of a football, but flatter. She wiped it over carefully with her bare hands and examined it closely.

'There is something engraved on it!' Careful rubbing with a handful of grass revealed a small inscription:

'E.M. 1844-1870'

'Do you think someone is buried here?' Ashley asked.

'I suppose someone could be buried here, but highly unusual. Most people would use the local churchyard,' Brian mused.

'Perhaps it was a murder or something bad,' Ashley conjectured.

'I doubt a murderer would carve a headstone or make a proper grave. I think it more likely something bad has happened. Perhaps an infectious disease or an accident, there could be other explanations. It now seems very odd that we have never, ever seen anyone use these houses. It's as if the place is being avoided.' Brian too was intrigued by the discovery, 'It wouldn't be hard to find out who owns the block. It would be on public record. The Council may have some information about the grave too, but I haven't got the time to look into the matter.'

'There is no reason I can't ask a few questions,' Ashley offered, 'it would give me something interesting to do while you are away.'

They both agreed to go home that afternoon. There was something unsettling about finding the grave. Rocky Bay had lost some of its allure. Sea, sex and sunshine had been overshadowed by Ashley's narrow escape in the rock pool and now a mystery connected with the house next door.

'You are very quiet,' Ashley commented, on their way home.

'I don't want to go to Mt. Gambier. I don't want to leave you alone, I feel apprehensive for your safety,' Brian was not usually concerned with hunches or premonitions, he was more practical.

'I have decided to stay at Light House until you return,' she sounded serenely positive. 'I have a bit of bookwork to do, Chris is there should I need a doctor, Stella will provide me with meals and I have company should I feel lonely. Also, I am in the city and central to all the records I need to investigate the two houses. As well I have Helen to go to for advice if I get stuck!'

'Well!' he said, 'It seems I am not at all necessary.'

'Yes, you are, you are all that is necessary. I am just trying to convince you that I will be safe in Light House.'

Ashley may have thought she had convinced Brian she would be safe at Light House, but she was mistaken. He was uneasy for the entire time spent in Mt. Gambier.

As soon as the job was wrapped up, instead of staying for a relaxing dinner, and travelling next morning, at Brian's request they took the night flight home.

'I nearly lost Ashley recently,' he confided to Jack and elaborated on the details, 'And, I worry about her staying at Light House.'

'Why does she have to stay there?' Jack was perplexed. He knew Ashley worked at Light House, but surely, they wouldn't need the money, Brian was a successful lawyer.

'She owns it,' Brian replied, 'she has developed it into a nice business.' Brian felt proud of her achievement. 'She runs it all from a little office she has set up in her own flat and she wants to stay there to catch up on a few things. I know she will be safe, but I would prefer her to stay at our home.'

'Whereabouts is Light House?' Jack asked.

'Palmer Street,' Brian replied, 'not far from Syms Simcock's offices.'

Jack was flabbergasted. It was right in the middle of the blue-chip centre of the city. It must be worth several million dollars. Light

House would be a perfect location for his group of companies to set up Head Office.

The plane landed and the men each took a taxi to their separate homes.

Light House was in darkness when Brian arrived. Once inside the automatic interior lights came on and he let himself into Ashley's apartment. That was only lit by a lamp. He looked at his wrist watch it was eleven o'clock, not quite her bedtime yet.

'Ashley,' he called softly, and there she was lying flat on her back on her bed, looking out of this world beautiful, with her hands clasped just under her breast. She was wearing white silk pyjamas that he knew she kept here in her apartment. She had bought some for him, but he had never worn them. The filmy white curtains moved slightly in the mild night air coming in from the window and there was a fragrance of lavender and roses.

She looked like she was 'dreaming' as she had described to him at one time and he dared not waken her, she had described the frightening consequences of being disturbed.

He went into the bathroom and the bathwater was still warm, it still smelt faintly of lavender and roses. On the bench was a pot of herbal tea and her Valerian drops.

On impulse he decided to join her, he was going to 'dream' too. He stripped off his clothes and put them on a chair. He poured some tea into her used cup, added a few Valerian drops, then a few more for good measure. The bathwater was cool, so he added more hot water and more lavender oil. Then he sank down into the bath and let the hot water soak away his tensions.

To his surprise it did, more quickly than expected. His relaxation may have been something to do with the herbal tea, but he discounted that idea because he didn't like the taste and took very little. When the water started to feel cool, he got out of the bath, dried himself, put on the silk pyjamas. They felt delightful against his skin and set him wondering why he had never before tried them on.

He hesitated before he climbed into the four-poster bed, knowing she was superstitious about it, but he reasoned he couldn't wake her, there wasn't another bed in the flat and he was very, very tired.

Hours and hours later, after the most sublime rest, he woke up to find Ashley gazing down at him looking absolutely amazed.

'Why are you here?' she demanded.

'We finished early and came home. I phoned, but couldn't get connected, so I came straight here. You were asleep. I know not to wake you. I had some of your tea, which tastes awful, got into your bath, which was lovely, put on these pyjamas, which I like, thank you very much and got into bed alongside you which is my right, in case you may have forgotten, because I was extremely tired.'

'Did we make love?' she asked.

'No! Of course not! It's against the rules. Silly ones if you ask me.'

'Are you sure?' she asked, still doubtful.

'I can assure you we didn't. You were asleep and I don't impose myself upon sleeping women.' There was a small silence.

'Why are we having this conversation?' he wanted to know.

'I got a shock to wake up and see you there. You know I have been paranoid about us sleeping together in this apartment from the beginning, but maybe there is an explanation. Do you want to hear what I have found out?'

'No, not really, I just want you to welcome me home, but if I must hear it I will.' Brian was more relaxed than he could ever remember and so happy just to be with Ashley.

'I spoke frankly to Helen Gilbertson about the Harpers, the Sisters of Light, Light House and the grave,' Ashley started immediately, revealing she was bursting to share her news.

'She suggested using the firm's Librarian, who knows where to look for everything, and who was absolutely marvellous. She used public records of course, but also records of old newspapers that are in the archives. Being prominent, the family was often mentioned in the social notes, or gossip columns.

The Harpers were a wealthy, ambitious family, prominent in local government and with an eye to a seat in the State government. They came out from England as settlers and purchased a large area of land in the Willunga area where they established almond orchards.

Aubrey Cyrus the youngest son chose to go into business, he had married a wealthy widow and he used her capital to build imposing business premises here in Adelaide. He saw there was a huge need for information in those early days and set himself up as an importer of law books, religious material and artefacts.

Adelaide was the capital city of The New Experimental British Colony of South Australia, later becoming unofficially known as the City of Churches, not for the number of buildings but for the number of different religions that prospered here. South Australia was the only state whose population was drawn from free settlers and not convicts.

Ships sailed back and forth to England and Aubrey sailed back on one of these to establish contacts and buy the stock he intended to continue to import. It was on his first trip back he met, in London, the sisters Phoebe and Eloise Marmont, who belonged to an Order named the Sisters of Light. They were nursing nuns, skilled in medicine and hospital care, making their way to St Catherine's Abbey on the far south coast of Greece. They thought of themselves as pioneers and wanted to take the Sisterhood to the islands of Greece where they thought to do much good.

They were staying at the same guesthouse as Aubrey. The two women were very different from each other. The older, smaller one was dark haired, dark eyed and intense. The younger one was lighter in colour and manner; they each had a 'presence'.

They knew, without being told, Aubrey was married. They knew he was from the 'New Land' before he mentioned it. Aubrey convinced them to bring the Sisterhood to Adelaide, instead of taking it to the Greek Isles, he felt sure his business and their service to the community would prosper side by side. He was proven to be right.

All three travelled to Australia on the same ship.

On arrival they set up 'The Sisters of Light – Natural and Spiritual Healthcare for

Women', in rooms provided by Aubrey. He allotted them two rooms on the first floor of his warehouse, to practise their particular brand of healing, spiritual and physical, plus the attic for their personal habitation. He also named the building 'Light House' to give their business more presence.

All three prospered for about ten years until Aubrey's fascination with Eloise, which had long been whispered about, became very apparent. There was a huge scandal and overnight the two Sisters disappeared, clearing out their bank accounts, taking with them what they could. There was a rumour they were seen in the Willunga area, but no confirmation. Several months later Phoebe was seen, alone, boarding a ship, but again no confirmation.

As far as Rocky Bay is concerned, the Council sub-divided it into two blocks. One was purchased by Aubrey Cyrus Harper in 1860, the other remained unsold until your father bought it in 1953. Aubrey had the two little houses built and one can only assume they were meant to be a separate house each for the sisters.' Ashley finished her long recital, anxious for Brian's re-action.

'I still think it's all circumstantial, but I understand your point. You think you are the descendent of Eloise Marmont and Aubrey Cyrus Harper, whose illegitimate daughter is the foundling child and your great grandmother.'

'Yes,' Ashley's face was alight with excitement.

'It also means that if my Mother is a Harper descendant of that particular family, we are probably related,' Brian stated flatly.

'What does that mean now?' asked a puzzled Ashley.

'It means our marriage will be annulled because it is illegal!' Brian teased.

'No!' cried Ashley, very upset.

'I was only teasing,' immediately contrite. 'In fact, I believe first cousins can be married now, so we are quite safe.' Brian was pleased to get that matter sorted out. He had other things on his mind.

'There is something else the Librarian found out. The block of land is available for sale for the amount of unpaid taxes due. If we bought the block, we could have the body exhumed and its DNA checked. That would answer any questions.' Ashley wasn't giving in.

'I will do anything you want,' said Brian, 'Give me your orders and I will see to it. Now that you have solved the mystery of the 'foundling' and all presumed curses are dispelled, I would like you to welcome me home. Here and now, in this bed that has been forbidden territory for seven years.'

'Do you agree?' he coaxed, drawing her close.

'I'm not sure,' she whispered.

'Must I drive us to my place, as we are, in our matching pyjamas, each of us scented with lavender and roses?

'Don't be silly!'

'I'm not silly, I'm desperate.'

'Me too,' she laughed, 'and for some unknown reason I am no longer afraid.'

CHAPTER 15
The Vigil

Nine months later Ashley and Brian were parents of a 2.7 kilo-gram baby girl whom they named Gina Ashley Preston Moore. Ashley had wanted to name the child Angelina after her mother. Brian, nervous for Ashley and testy for the entire nine months, wanted nothing more to do with angels and wouldn't agree.

Completely opposite Brian's reaction, pregnancy agreed with Ashley. She was calm, sweet tempered and blooming with good health. She held no fear of childbirth and when the time came for her to go to hospital, Christine Forrest prescribed a sedative for Brian.

Delivery of the child was relatively easy. Brian wasn't interested in the baby, only that Ashley was safe. Later on, when the baby had been cleaned up and put with the mother and he saw them both together, unstoppable tears ran down his face.

'Thank God, that's over!' he said unevenly, 'I never want that experience again!'

Life wasn't the same after Gina arrived, at their home or at Light House. The baby was a good little thing, but it took all of Ashley's energy to care for it, which she found depressing.

Marion arrived more often to 'help out' but found nothing to do, they already had regular people employed to do the laundry, and general housework. Marion was annoyed and thought Brian spoilt Ashley, adding that to her list of grievances.

'I'm at my wit's end,' Brian admitted to Christine Forest, 'I can see she is not improving and I don't know what to do!'

'All her tests are normal. There are no obvious signs of abnormality. I have suggested she consults a Diagnostic Physician but she has declined to go. I can only suggest you take her away for a holiday.' Christine had offered her professional opinion and could see it didn't answer Brian's problem.

'What do you think about us going to Sydney for a time?' He started off the suggestion carefully. 'I would like to take Gina to visit Forbes and Anna. They must be curious to see our baby and Anna is the only female of your acquaintance, who could talk to you as a mother.' Brian hoped Ashley would agree.

She did and they spent a lovely week in Sydney. Anna and Ashley spent hours discussing all things maternal. Brian and Forbes conversation explored the options of disposing of Light House, should Ashley ever wish to relinquish her property.

Helen quickly got onto the job of purchasing the allotment at Rocky Bay. Once Council became aware of an unregistered grave on the site, they assumed responsibility for the exhumation. When they were apprised of the suspicions of the purchaser as to the corpse's identity and the purchaser's willingness to cover the cost, should their suspicions prove correct, Council was happy to move the investigation along swiftly.

Robert Moore took great interest in the proposed exhumation process and wanted to be there when it happened. Marion confirmed her grandfather was Charles James Symonds Harper, son of Aubrey Cyrus. She felt important and wanted to witness the exhumation too.

Ashley was the one most affected. She had found the grave and she was about to find out if the body was that of her great-grandmother.

'I don't know what to do,' Brian admitted to Ashley. 'I can't tell them they are not welcome in their own house. I don't mind Dad, but Mum is sure to say something to offend you,' he looked so down and depressed, Ashley's heart softened.

'Brian,' she said softly, I love you, dearly and forever. I want your parents to come to Rocky Bay. We three have our little room upstairs. You once said you always brought your treasures to that room, well, now you have another one to tuck away.'

The exhumation was an anti-climax. Three Council gravediggers arrived early one morning. They worked solidly stopping only for 'smoko' then not long afterwards struck the casket. It was raised without too much difficulty, but they did not have permission to open it.

Brian phoned his contact at the Council, who said a Supervisor would be sent to the site, but it would take a few hours. There was nothing to do but wait. The gravediggers went home and everyone else sat around and waited. Brian and Robert inspected the casket several times, but there was no way for them to open it without doing some sort of damage.

Finally, the Supervisor arrived, Brian signed the papers and the casket was prised open. Death is an ugly sight. It shook Robert and Marion and horrified Ashley and Brian.

To a layman there was no telling if the skeleton was male or female, only the fact it appeared to be small would one guess it to be female. They replaced the lid and it was sent to the Council who would see to it being reburied in the local Churchyard after samples were sent off for DNA testing. Brian and his father backfilled the hole and they all packed up and went home.

It took weeks for the DNA results to become known but eventually they received the notification that Ashley's DNA was a match. Ashley knew now that her great grandmother was the foundling baby left on the doorstep of the Adelaide Children's Home back in 1870.

It should have pleased her to know that the foundling had found a nice useful life at the Children's Home and then much later with Reverend Samuels, although she had died in childbirth. Her own mother happily married a young man whom she loved dearly. Sadly, Ashley's parents were taken prematurely in a car accident, but Ashley had survived that accident and was happily married to a man whom she loved and who loved her in return. It should have pleased her to be alive and well, but instead it cast her down.

Brian called into Light House to pick her up as usual. She had spent the day there to show off little Gina and to do a bit of book work. They were both on the four-poster bed, Ashley asleep, and the baby just awake. Gina saw Brian and began kicking excitedly wanting to be picked up. He did that and wondered what he should do about Ashley. He touched her gently and was shocked to discover she was cold.

Something worse than dread washed over him, he felt paralysed. He put the baby back in her cot, left the apartment and knocked on Christine Forrest's door. One look at his face told her something was dreadfully wrong.

'It's Ashley,' his voice was muted, he could hardly speak. Grabbing her bag, she hurried with him to his apartment. She felt for a pulse, used her stethoscope around her heart and called an ambulance citing 'utmost emergency'. She looked at Brian who hadn't spoken, who couldn't speak. He was dumb, numb and petrified.

The ambulance crew arrived; other apartment dwellers emerged. Helen picked up Gina who was by now, bawling loudly. Brian went in the ambulance with Ashley. His world had collapsed. He sat around in the hospital, waiting. A big bloke came out from somewhere dressed in a white theatre gown. He introduced himself as the doctor.

'I'm very sorry,' he said, 'it was too late.'

'Too late,' Brian repeated vaguely.

'Your wife has passed away, I am sorry.'

'We think an epileptic event has brought on a heart attack. Has your wife had epilepsy before?'

'No! She 'dreams'! He made an effort to pull himself together. 'She has warned me not to wake her if she is asleep because she may be 'dreaming.' She says sometimes she feels she can't get back into her body, if she is awakened suddenly.' Brian was becoming distraught again.

'Has she had these dreams recently' asked the medic.

'No, I don't believe so,' Brian felt outside of himself, he could hear the subdued busyness of a hospital but it seemed unreal. The Doctor was talking, but Brian didn't hear.

'May I see her?' he asked, interrupting whatever information the doctor was trying to impart. They took him to a curtained cubicle where Ashley lay neatly tucked into a white bed, her arms outside of the covers. He kissed her hair, her brow, her closed eyes, her cold lips and her lifeless hand. He held it against his cheek until it was wet with his tears. He tried to dry it with his handkerchief, but that was wet too. His grief was unbearable, and unbearable to watch.

Christine Forrest and the doctor left him alone. Christine was able to answer most of the doctor's questions and she authorised the removal of the body to the mortuary. She also took the responsibility of seeing that Brian was given a sedative to help him cope.

'Mr. Moore briefly explained that she has 'dreams', which sound to me like a type of 'night epilepsy'. A sudden disturbance could have triggered the heart attack. He said he was always careful not to waken her suddenly and he also said the mother and child were both together on their bed when he found them. It is quite probable that the baby woke up, started crying and that set off this whole tragedy. I will investigate along these lines, because as you know, a death so soon after admittance to a hospital becomes a matter for the Coroner and they will want full details.'

'Epilepsy was never mentioned to me, or dreaming for that matter. I recall once she was blue around the lips and I wanted to investigate. She flatly refused a blood test or any investigation what-so-ever. The only treatment she requested was for birth control.' Christine felt upset. She felt she had been made to appear a careless physician.

'I wouldn't want to be the one to suggest the theory to Brian that the child could have triggered Ashley's heart attack,' Christine answered, 'it could mar his relationship with his daughter for the rest of his life.'

'I will still have to investigate along those lines and leave it to the Coroner to report his findings,' said the hospital doctor.

Brian was in a vacuum. He remembered nothing of leaving the hospital or being taken back to Light House.

He was surprised to find Helen looking after Gina. He had forgotten about the baby completely.

'Would you like me to phone your parents, Brian?' Helen suggested kindly. 'They would probably be pleased to care for little Gina until you can work something out.'

'Whatever!' he said dully.

'You will have to pull yourself together!' Helen snapped. 'You fathered the child and you have to care for her, or arrange for someone else to look after her, whether you want to or not!'

He didn't answer Helen. He just looked at her for a few minutes. Perhaps her words were just starting to sink in, whatever the reason, he picked up the telephone and asked to speak to his father. He quietly explained what had happened and arranged to meet them at their house in about an hour. Then he collected the baby's carry cot, grabbed whatever things he thought she needed and asked Helen if she would mind bringing the child down to his car.

'Would you like me to come with you?' she asked, she didn't want to hand the baby over but knew she must.

'No thanks, Helen' he quickly replied,' but I would like to thank you for your help this evening.' He felt cold, like an automaton, there were things to do and he did them.

His parents were waiting for him. They had prepared a cot for Gina, having baby furniture in their spare room for 'hoped for' grand-children. Robert poured Brian a stiff scotch and listened attentively as Brian described the events of the night as well as he could.

Brian phoned Charles from his father's house and then Forbes. It was a half hour off midnight, less than five hours since he had arrived at Light House from work, looking forward to another delicious evening with Ashley and little Gina, who had only just started to make a place for herself in his heart.

The funeral came and passed with Brian in a vacuum, only dimly aware of it happening. Forbes gave a touching eulogy and so too did Charles and Helen.

As soon as it was over, he left town without explanation to anyone. He used his old car, the one he had given to Ashley. He drove to Glenbourne, stopping at the place where Ashley's parents had died. It clearly was a dangerous sweep of a bend and he spent some time observing the traffic before continuing.

He booked into a motel and over the next few days he looked up the house where Ashley was raised with Max and Ellen. It was still a substantial well cared for home and surrounded by other equally substantial houses. Their shops were not so easily identified. Max's tailoring shop was now a cafe, he entered and ordered coffee. He didn't feel like eating, in fact hadn't eaten a meal since leaving Adelaide.

Aunt Ellen's haberdashery was now a hardware outlet. He stayed around Glenbourne for a few days content to walk around and absorb the atmosphere. He visited the primary school she attended and sat around watching the youngsters in the playground, until a policeman came up and asked why he was watching the children.

He hadn't showered or shaved since he left home, so he bought himself jeans, sweater and some underwear, returned to his motel to bathe and shave and change clothes. He took his discarded clothes to a dry-cleaners and laundry. That night he ate a meal in the motel dining room and had a better night's sleep.

Next day he moved on to Sydney. His first stop was St. Anne's College where he had made an appointment with the Headmistress. At least his freshly cleaned clothes were smart, but he had lost so much weight they fitted poorly. The Headmistress had referred to their records and reported Ashley's school history exactly as Ashley had described it, adding that she had been an excellent student, but shy, withdrawn and not at all confident about mixing with other students. There was no record of illness, or of doctors' referrals.

Forbes and Anna welcomed him like a long-lost son almost shattering his composure. They were aghast at his haggard appearance, but discreetly made no mention of it. Brian told them what he had been doing for the past few weeks. Trying to get a feel of the environment from whence Ashley came, and asking about her health at her old school.

'I thought they may have mentioned the 'dreaming,' Brian explained. 'Ashley told me she had been seen many doctors over the years but with no result.' He also described how they had 'met'. 'She told me she was living with you and Anna at the time so would have been about sixteen. She also said she kept her 'dreaming' a secret.'

'I know Max and Ellen were anxious about Ashley 'seeing people' in her dreams and took her to various doctors, but nothing came of it. I think it was suggested it may have been a slight disorder associated with puberty and would pass. It was the reason we agreed to have her live with us, one we never regretted. Our experience of having her live with us was delightful. We took pride in her work at school and she fitted into our home and my office seamlessly. All of my staff loved her, and were heartbroken when I told them the news. Anna and I never saw anything lacking or alarming health wise, and we loved her as if she were our own.' Forbes sighed deeply, wishing he could say something to ease Brian's pain but was wise enough to know a little practical comfort would help a lot more.

'You are very welcome to stay with us for however long you would like,' he suggested. 'Perhaps you would like to use her room upstairs. It's quiet, has nice views and has its own exit. Ashley used to often go down to the little beach for a swim. I would lend you some togs, but mine would be too big.'

Brian gratefully accepted the invitation. There was room in Forbes garage for his car and he found a pair of swim togs in the boot of his car when he was collecting his luggage.

'We usually gather about seven for drinks, dinner is at seven thirty,' Forbes explained as he left Brian standing just inside the doorway of Ashley's old room.

Brian moved inside and closed the door. It was a long room with windows all around one side and both ends, taking advantage of the lovely harbour views in the area. There was furniture at one end for reading and writing and her bed at the other. He became aware of a sense of peacefulness as he walked around touching things. She had lived here! It was hard to absorb but it felt like a balm to his spirit.

Sitting on the edge of her bed he remembered she had told him she was sixteen when they 'met' in her dream. This was the bed where she would have had that psychic experience. He had been twenty-six at the time. The meeting had brought a seismic shift to his life that changed it for the better. Ten years later she walked into his office, this time in reality. The dream had been forgotten, but not Ashley. She brought with her a long period of unimagined bliss. A wave of despair washed over him as he realised finally, she was gone and he alone, with only a baby to love. He lay down on the bed completely exhausted and slept.

He slept for the remainder of the day, all night and most of the next day appearing for 'drinks' at seven, and apologising for being twenty-four hours late.

Next morning, rising early, he put on his swimmers, let himself out of the exit door of

Ashley's room, went down the wooden stairs, found the path to the beach and took an invigorating swim in the calm waters of the Harbour. It was what he imagined Ashley would have done and had to admit it made him feel physically and emotionally stronger. He stayed a few days longer soaking up the comfort until thoughts of home started to intrude on his rest, and he knew he should move on.

After thanking Anna and Forbes for their generous hospitality he was about to leave when Forbes took him aside.

'I have been thinking of the Angels,' he began, which immediately grabbed Brian's attention.

'If they bother you at all, I would suggest you donate them to the Migration Museum, Adelaide has a very interesting migration story. There is bound to be interest from a Historical Society too. From what I understand Light House became notorious at one stage of its history and they would make for an interesting exhibit.' Brian thanked him for the suggestion. Forbes could see his advice was well received.

Back home in Adelaide after a long two-day drive, stopping overnight in a motel to make sure he would be fresh enough cope with his mother, he arrived at his parent's house late afternoon. Brian hadn't bothered to make any contact at all with his mother and he expected her to take issue with his thoughtlessness.

'Gina has been very good,' said Marion, 'but caring for a baby fulltime is very tiring for me. I hope you understand.'

'I do, completely. I phoned Charles last night from my motel and I will be starting back at work on Monday. I will take Gina off your hands as of now if you like, I am ready,' Brian replied quietly.

'I am so glad you are ready!' She sarcastically replied, 'what about me! I've not got her things packed or her food organised. Why could you not have phoned me last night, or some other time? You have been gone nearly a month without one word!' Marion was rightly incensed.

'I had some sort of a break-down. I ended up in Sydney. Forbes had a chat with his doctor.

I will go and see someone soon, I promise. Last night by the time I finished with Charles it was much too late to phone.' Brian could see his mother was reasonably mollified.

'Come with me,' said Robert gently, taking advantage of a lull in the conversation, 'and have a look at Miss Gina, she is a prize.'

She was in her cot playing prettily with a rattle. Bright blue eyes registered alarm when she saw a stranger's face come close. She looked to Robert for reassurance. Gina was the living image of Ashley and seeing it, his heart fell in pieces again.

'We will miss her,' Marion said when they were ready to go. 'She is a delightful little thing. Ring me at any time if you are in trouble,' her voice broke and seeing her emotion, Brian hugged his mother closely. It touched him more than he expected.

Robert and Marion stood side by side waving him goodbye until he was out of sight.

Brian found his home just as he had left it, smart, luxurious, cold and empty. Gina was asleep in her car capsule. He carried the baby in carefully and managed to transfer her to the cot without causing a disturbance.

Marion had provided an early dinner for them all and settled Gina down with a bottle not long before Brian left.

'She is a good little sleeper,' she said, 'she has been sleeping through the night, not waking until early morning.'

Brian found her just the opposite. He was up every hour, attending to the slightest squeak or squawk. She couldn't settle simply because of unfamiliar hands and voice and smell. Finally, exhaustion demanded sleep and she succumbed long enough to build up enough energy for another protest.

Helen Gilbertson had been brought up to date with Brian's movements by Charles, who phoned her at her flat. Helen phoned Brian who sounded terse, impatient and angry. She knew him well and worried about the child.

'I don't care what sort of reception I get,' she told her mother Moira, 'the baby isn't responsible for his troubles. I'm going to see that she is alright!'

It was almost lunch-time when Helen arrived. Standing at the front door she could hear a commotion inside the house. The baby was screaming hysterically, she heard Brian shouting.

'I know you want your Mama! I do too, but she has gone!'

There was a tiny silence and Helen took the opportunity to knock loudly on the front door. She heard quick angry footsteps coming up the passage, the door was savagely opened and Brian stood there, splattered with baby-food and glowering. She stood for a moment taking in the situation.

'It looks like she's got your temper!' Helen remarked drily, pushing past him and heading straight for the kitchen, she knew the house well.

'What are you doing here?' he asked following her down the passage.

'I wanted to see Gina,' she said holding out her arms to the still sobbing child, who miraculously stopped crying and held up her little arms. Helen held her close, ignoring the mess, whispering silly things and calming the baby down. Brian watched them for a few minutes, no doubt taking notes, before starting on cleaning up the kitchen.

'Where do you bathe and change her?' she asked, and Brian showed her Gina's room where everything necessary was laid out close to hand.

'Ashley thought of everything when she refurbished your house,' Helen remarked, but Brian only nodded in agreement. He couldn't talk about Ashley and quickly disappeared to spruce up himself.

About an hour later the baby had taken some lunch and was contentedly sucking on her bottle. They each had a ham sandwich which Brian prepared, and a glass of wine.

'What are you proposing to do about caring for Gina?' it was the obvious question to ask and needed to be discussed.

'Mum, probably, I haven't got much further than that. The other option is to hire a Nanny.'

'I would love to be her Nanny,' Helen said softly, looking at Gina who was nearly asleep on the couch beside her.

'You!' Brian couldn't disguise his surprise.

'I've always wanted a child,' she quietly confessed.

'Are you really serious?'

'I wouldn't say that as a joke,' she replied.

'Why haven't you married?' Brian realised it was too personal, but the question was out before he had thought about it.

'I haven't been asked,' she answered.

'I have been in love though,' she admitted, seeing his embarrassment and wanting to put him at ease. 'It was the type of love that knocks you off your feet, so that nothing else in the world matters! You know what I mean. I saw it happen between you and Ashley!'

'What happened?' he had to ask.

'He met someone else,' she said quietly and Brian could see it still hurt.

'A Nanny wouldn't pay anything like your salary,' Brian was getting back to business. He liked the idea of Helen as Gina's Nanny. He could rely on her completely.

'Perhaps we could arrange something. First of all, I want Gina to be raised in this

house. She is to be in no doubt it is her home.'
He thought for a moment then continued,

'Ashley did the administration work for Light House. Perhaps you could take that over and work it in with your Nanny duties. Ashley was doing that before she died.' He stopped. He didn't want to go on. After a while he resumed.

'Think about it, Helen. The two jobs could more than match your salary and you would be paid by Light House. We can work out details later.'

That is what happened, as soon as it could be properly arranged, and it worked out well. Gina's Nanny came to live at Gina's house. Brian was then free to go away on business whenever necessary, or for when he wanted to stay in Light House. Gina's Nanny also had the foresight and plain common-sense to include Gina's grandparents in Gina's life. She made sure of this by arranging frequent visits to Gina's grandparent's home and inviting them back to Brian's place in return. She did this by taking advantage of the fact that Brian's Dad still took care of much of the gardening at

Brian's place, so Gina's Nanny always made sure Brian's Mum came too, to visit the infant, and that there was a nice simple lunch available for them all to enjoy.

When the time came, Gina's Nanny and Grandparents were always invited to school concerts, sports days and open days to be a visible part of Gina's life.

Helen also was always available when there was entertaining to do. The second spare bedroom became her room and she and Gina used the little sitting room for study and talking and discussion. Brian was staying more and more often at Light House, but he was confident Gina was safe and well-guarded.

The time came for Gina to go to university and she chose medicine. She had grown into a beautiful young woman, not at all like her mother whom she had so strongly resembled as a child. She looked more like Brian, lovely glossy brown hair, keen grey/green eyes, finely shaped nose and sweet lips. She graduated at twenty-four and became an intern. Her first serious boy-friend did not meet Brian's approval.

Jeremy was not Brian's idea of a suitable man for his daughter. He had taken a strong interest in her development all her life and was proud of the young woman she had become, only to be disappointed in her choice of a male friend.

Helen retired from her job as companion/housekeeper as soon as Gina graduated and started her internship. Gina was required to live at the hospital, so Helen moved back into Light House, continuing to do its bookwork. She also continued to attend to anything Brian required to be done at his home where entertainment was concerned.

Brian eventually retired as Managing Partner of Syms, Simcock, but continued on as a Consultant. Often, he stayed overnight at Light House during the week because it was more convenient and less tiring than driving home to an empty house.

His friendship with Jack Henderson survived the years and they were now on the brink of launching the re-development of Light House. Jack had long envisaged a grand head office on the site, but business had ebbed for a few years and those plans were set aside. The plans had now resurfaced, had been re-drawn and submitted to Council. Pre-sale of office space, show-room space and pent-house space had commenced and Brian decided it was time he handed over the project to a younger man.

He chose James Sinclair, whose career he had been watching for several years.

'Hi Gina, its Dad,' he said, when she eventually answered her phone. He had tried un-successfully several times during the day but she was rostered for 'emergency' duty therefore frequently unavailable.

'I would like you to have dinner with me tonight at Ziggy's place. I have something important to tell you and someone I want you to meet,' Brian had to be careful of the way he tried to introduce her to his colleagues, she had taken exception to a couple of the fine young men he had introduced, and accused him of trying to run her life.

'Why do I have to meet this person?' She queried, already argumentative.

'Because you as my heiress, will need some guidance when I am gone. I am clearing up my estate now and intend appointing someone I can trust to continue my work.'

'Where are you going?' she asked perplexed.

'No further than Rocky Bay at the moment. I have vague plans of building another house on our spare block of land. I am retiring.'

Gina was more than surprised to hear her father was going into retirement. She had never thought of him becoming tired of his work. He was a little grey around the temples, but it was an attractive greying. It made her wonder why he never re-married. She had often wished he and Helen would marry. Between them they had made good parents, but it would have been nicer if they were proper parents.

Brian was at the table when Gina arrived in a taxi. He stood up waiting for her to sit down, she liked his old-fashioned manners. He was pleased to see she looked smartly dressed. Gina, if she thought he was match-making, had often presented herself unattractively.

'Your colleague is late!' she remarked,

thinking that all the other prospects Brian had introduced were ready and waiting, perhaps this really was just business.

'He will be here soon, his girlfriend will be dropping him off,' Brian was pleased she had noticed. He was using another strategy tonight. James Sinclair was something like his old friend Mike in his bachelor days, lots of glamorous girlfriends until the right one came along.

'Here he comes now,' he said, indicating outside the window. A smart red sports car was pulling up. It was driven by a very glamorous young, blonde woman. James leaned across, kissed her, they exchanged a few words and then he strode towards the restaurant.

Brian introduced James to Gina.

Ziggy Jnr. arrived with the champagne Brian had ordered and began pouring it out. They raised their glasses.

'Here's to brand new life,' Brian toasted.

James and Gina both assumed he meant his retirement, but Brian had seen that immediate infinitesimal spark between them both and that was the precise moment he knew his job was done.

CHAPTER 16
The Glory

Dinner was everything Brian hoped it would be. The meal was excellent, conversation easy, and importantly, the two young people were comfortable with each other. James was first to leave and Brian suggested Gina come back to Light House with him, as there was something he wanted to explain.

'What are you going to do with the angels?' she asked when they had settled comfortably in the lounge.

'That is what I want to talk about,' Brian was pleased she raised the subject.

'Forbes suggested, many years ago, that I should donate them to the Museum. He had a good point, they would have made a titillating exhibit, but I am more of a romantic than Forbes ever was, bless his soul. I think they have been sequestered long enough. They have paid for their sins, whatever they were and shall be freed to do the work for which they were originally intended. As such, they will be the only decorative items in the Prayer Room in the re-developed 'Light House'.

Brian took a sip of his champagne; it was the brand Ashley liked and he always kept a supply of it on hand. He still had that feeling of 'a job completed' that came over him in the restaurant and he luxuriated in it, at the same time answering Gina's questions that came thick and fast.

'Mike has done an amazing job of the building,' he interrupted her inquisition to get on with his tale at his own pace. 'He excelled himself when I asked his advice about the angels. He had never seen them, but he knew of the peculiar way I 'met' your mother. When I showed them to him and told him what I know of their history he came up with the idea of a prayer room. Non-denominational, of course, there will be nothing in it except a semi-circle of benches and prayer rail in an empty carpeted sunken area. You will be able to sit, kneel or prostrate yourself, as is your preference.

He also suggested having them professionally restored and has sought advice from our Art Gallery. Not that they are damaged in any way, but they have been around for a long time and are dulled from exposure to general atmospheric conditions. They would have been part of the décor in Phoebe's and Eloise's meeting room in Light House, from when they first arrived in here Adelaide and would have been left behind in the empty building, when the sisters had to flee. They have been there ever since.

Mike suggests that the Angels, as symbols of love, peace and hope for us all, will be the focal point of the Prayer Room. They will stand either side of a great window that will be placed at a height and angle that captures no landscape, only the eastern sky. He further suggests that the carpet in the prayer area should be blue, to compliment the sky view.'

Gina thought her father seemed a little emotional. Giving up his work, as well as losing control of Light House, would be a huge wrench. She suddenly realised it was all he had for comfort after the loss of her mother.

'So, what is the story about the angels, Dad? They have been in my life forever and I have accepted them, but I don't really know why they are here.' Gina was suddenly curious.

'They were gifted to Phoebe and Eloise Marmont from Aubrey Cyrus Harper, probably to enhance the premises where they would practise their calling. The two women belonged to a nursing sisterhood called 'The Sisters of Light'. Aubrey was in love with Eloise. When he discovered they were to have a child, he had two little houses built on a piece of land he owned at Rocky Bay, we assume one for him and Eloise and the other for Phoebe. We further assume it was where they planned to wait out the term of Eloise's pregnancy, they are small houses, no more than shacks, really.

In my private opinion, all three planned to re-settle elsewhere as soon as the baby was born.' Brian took another sip of champagne.

'It must have been difficult for the two women to exist at Rocky Bay,' he continued, 'they would have relied on him to bring supplies, or make do with their little garden and a bit of fishing. Eloise died giving birth, we guess, because Phoebe was sighted alone, several months after they fled from Adelaide, boarding a ship.

I can well imagine Aubrey's devastation. If he loved Eloise as I loved your mother he would have been out of his mind with grief. 'I was,' he quietly confessed, 'I can't remember your mother's funeral or the weeks afterwards,' he sat quietly contemplating his champagne.

'Anyway,' he continued, 'we also assume Phoebe and Eloise were trying to get to St. Catherine's Abbey, on an island off the southeast coast of Greece, the place to which they were originally travelling when they first met Aubrey.

After the scandal broke, Aubrey's business failed. They were unforgiving times and he would have been ostracized by society. The only asset he had left was Light House and to protect it from being sold off to creditors he put a ninety-nine-year Encumbrance on the property. I can't understand his reasoning here and can only imagine he was temporarily deranged. Either that, or he couldn't bear to part with all that was left of his love for Eloise.

The baby girl born at Rocky Bay had been left on the steps of an orphanage, she faced a destitute future. His wife and two children faced a bleak future too, as he had lost his reputation, as well as their fortune. I can understand the residual anger against Eloise and Aubrey that permeated the Harper family throughout subsequent generations.

How strange then, ninety-nine years later when the encumbrance expired, Ashley and I should see each other in what she called a 'psychic vision'.

Ashley is the great-grand daughter of Eloise Marmont and I am the great-grand son of Aubrey Cyrus Harper.

How strange that Ashley, through a series

of death and accident, was able to purchase Light House. How strange that on the day she first actually saw it she should walk into my office and into my life.' Brian suddenly felt very tired and spent. Gina noticed immediately and told him it was 'time he went to bed'.

'I'll give you no argument,' he said giving her the keys of his car. 'Take these and drive yourself to the hospital, you can bring it back tomorrow,' kissing her goodbye.

Alone with his memories, he straightened the couch cushions and picked up the glasses and champagne bottle. There was plenty of champagne left, so he poured himself another glass and took it to the bathroom, setting it down on the bench.

He turned on the taps to run a bath, and while it was filling, opened the bed and laid out his pyjamas, the white silk ones Ashley had bought for him long ago. He didn't make herbal tea, the taste wasn't to his liking but he did add a few drops of valerian to his champagne, he wanted to make sure he had a really good night's sleep.

He undressed, hung up his suit, left his other clothes on a chair, put a generous dash of lavender oil in the bath and lowered himself into the tub. It felt gloriously relaxing, better than ever before. The champagne tasted good too, he didn't even mind the taste of valerian. When the water cooled, he got out of the tub, dried himself, put on his pyjamas and gratefully stretched out in the soft comfortable bed.

Almost immediately he could feel a soft sea breeze, like the ones that waft around Rocky Bay. He drifted with the breeze. The sky seemed lighter and he recognised a delightful fragrance. It pierced his heart with exquisite precision.

He wanted to find the source of the perfume and was searching. He could see a vast distance, and in it a flutter of white. He strained to see as the white took shape. It was Ashley in her beach coat. That pierced his heart again.

He tried to call out her name, but his voice wouldn't come. He tried to run to her, but his legs wouldn't move. She saw him and smiled radiantly. It was like pure sunshine after a dark, dark storm.

He made a superhuman effort to reach her. His heart stopped, but it didn't matter, they were together.

———

Next day, Gina delivered the car as promised and found her father in the four-poster bed looking as if he had seen glory.

She closed his eyes and started to cry. She cried for some time. She cried for all the things she didn't know and for all the things she now would never know.

Calming down, she quietly made three phone calls, the Police, the Hospital and to James Sinclair.

Then she walked down to Helen Gilbertson's apartment and knocked on the door.

The End